TREASURE OF PANTHER PEAK

AILEEN KILGORE HENDERSON

ILLUSTRATIONS BY MARK COYLE

MILKWEED EDITIONS

© 1998, Text by Aileen Kilgore Henderson
© 1998, Illustrations by Mark Coyle
All rights reserved. Except for brief quotations in critical articles or reviews, no part of this book may be reproduced in any manner without prior written permission from the publisher: Milkweed Editions, 430 First Avenue North, Suite 400, Minneapolis, MN 55401
Distributed by Publishers Group West

Published 1998 by Milkweed Editions
Printed in Canada
Cover design by Tara Christopherson, Fruitful Results Design
Cover and interior illustrations by Mark Coyle
Interior design by Will Powers
The text of this book is set in ITC Stone Serif.
98 99 00 01 02   5 4 3 2 1
First Edition

Milkweed Editions is a not-for-profit publisher. We gratefully acknowledge support from Alliance for Reading Funders: Cray Research, a Silicon Graphics Company; Dayton Hudson Circle of Giving; Ecolab Foundation; Musser Fund; Jay and Rose Phillips Foundation; Rathmann Family Foundation; Target Stores; United Arts School and Partnership Funds. Other support has been provided by the Elmer L. and Eleanor J. Andersen Foundation; James Ford Bell Foundation; Bush Foundation; Dayton's, Mervyn's, and Target Stores by the Dayton Hudson Foundation; Doherty, Rumble & Butler Foundation; Dorsey and Whitney Foundation; General Mills Foundation; Honeywell Foundation; Jerome Foundation; McKnight Foundation; Minnesota State Arts Board through an appropriation by the Minnesota State Legislature; Creation and Presentation Programs of the National Endowment for the Arts; Norwest Foundation on behalf of Norwest Bank Minnesota, Norwest Investment Management & Trust, Lowry Hill, Norwest Investment Services, Inc.; Lawrence and Elizabeth Ann O'Shaughnessy Charitable Income Trust in honor of Lawrence M. O'Shaughnessy; Oswald Family Foundation; Piper Jaffray Companies, Inc.; Ritz Foundation; John and Beverly Rollwagen Fund of the Minneapolis Foundation; St. Paul Companies, Inc.; Star Tribune Foundation; James R. Thorpe Foundation; and generous individuals.

Library of Congress Cataloging-in-Publication Data

Henderson, Aileen.
    Treasure of Panther Peak / Aileen Kilgore Henderson ; illustrated by Mark Coyle. — 1st ed.
        p.   cm.
    Summary: Twelve-year-old Page and her mother travel all the way from Alabama to the rugged, isolated Big Bend National Park in Texas, where her mother gets a job teaching in a small school and where they start a new life away from Page's abusive father.
    ISBN 1-57131-618-3 (cloth). — ISBN 1-57131-619-1 (paper)
    [1. Mothers and daughters—Fiction.   2. Schools—Fiction.   3. Big Bend National Park (Texas)—Fiction.   4. Texas—Fiction.   5. Family violence—Fiction.]   I. Coyle, Mark, ill.   II. Title.
PZ7.H37874Tr 1998
[Fic]—dc21   98-21806
                                                                                CIP
                                                                                AC

This book is printed on acid-free paper.

To all the students who attended the school at Panther Junction in Big Bend National Park, Texas, during 1952–1954.

Treasure of Panther Peak

1

ALL NIGHT LONG as the train hurtled westward from Alabama, twelve-year-old Page Williams did not shut her angry eyes one time. She glared fixedly at the shiny black window, which looked back at her like a blank television screen.

The train had long since rocked through the big cities—New Orleans, Houston, San Antonio. Now, with daylight not far off, it clacked steadily across a rugged desert land, without lights of any kind, a land as lonely, it seemed to Page, as the wailing train whistle.

One reason for Page's anger lay ahead of them, a place called Panther Flat at the foot of the Ghost Mountains in the wild Big Bend country of Texas. Page had never been there. Her mother, Ellie, asleep in the seat beside her, had never been there either. But in Mom's suitcase was a brand new diploma tied with a red ribbon. It proclaimed that Ellie Williams, as of June 1953, had earned a Bachelor of Science degree from the state university that qualified her to teach. Now the two of them were on their way to Mom's first school, beyond the backside of nowhere.

But theirs was no ordinary train ride from one place to another. They were running away like fugitives, escaping from the house that had always been home to Page. In that house, a thousand miles behind them, was another reason for Page's anger--Dad—handsome, laughing, teasing Dad. Against her will, Page's mind projected onto the dark train window scenes from this past year, of Dad's sudden explosions of temper when he lashed out with hard fists to smash the china horses she kept on her dresser or the antique doll house Mom had inherited from her grandmother. Sometimes he threatened to kill himself. Other times he aimed his gun at her and Mom because, he said, they were plotting to commit him to the psychiatric hospital.

In her dresser drawer at home, where Page kept the broken china horses, she also kept a secret phone number Mom gave her. "It's Lorna's number, my friend at school," Mom said. "Call her if—if the time comes when you know I need help." Page felt embarrassed that Mom had told anybody about Dad. Even the two of them didn't talk about the bad times at home. Page memorized the number, but when the time came in the middle of a spring night when she had to dial Lorna, she was so terrified she couldn't remember it. She finally found the slip of paper under the china pieces but when she dialed, praying that Lorna would answer, she only had time to gasp, "Mom needs you—Ellie Williams, I mean. Please come!" before Dad stomped in and tore the phone out of the wall.

Lorna came for them where they waited in the alley behind their house. Page was in her pajamas, barefoot and shivering from more than cold. Mom held her broken glasses in place with one hand trying to

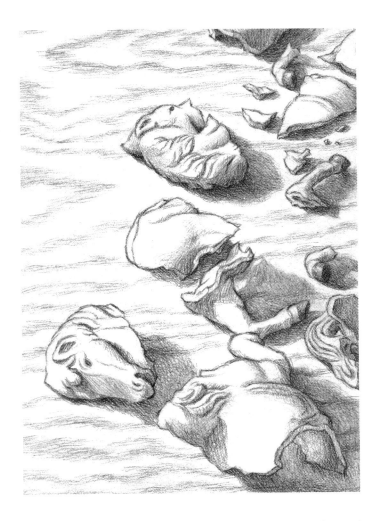

hide a blackened eye and the print of Dad's hand outlined in red across her cheek. They carried nothing
with them except Mom's purse.

In the days afterward, which they spent in Lorna's
back bedroom, Page's anger turned against her

mother. "If you'd quit school the way Dad wanted, everything would've been all right. It's your fault!" she had raged.

Mom's bruised eye looked like an ugly flower on her pale face. Page knew she was hurting, and not just physically. Yet shouting, "It's all your fault!" made Page feel better.

Mom replied slowly, as if thinking over each word before she spoke it, "I had to graduate so I can earn a living for us. Sooner or later, we would have had to leave, no matter what I did."

Lorna defended Mom in a no-nonsense voice. "Ellie did the right thing to leave a situation so dangerous for you both. It could have been deadly for her, as I've seen too many times."

Mom had explained to Page that Lorna, besides attending school, worked with the social welfare office in their town. She often helped women who were having a rough time at home. It was Lorna who found the teaching job at Panther Flat for Mom. Coming to the kitchen for breakfast one morning, Page overheard her saying, "It's a good setup for you, Ellie—the school board will pay your way to Panther Flat. I found out that the school is new, with an apartment built on for the teacher." She paused. "Of course, I understand the place is isolated, surrounded by a national park. But the farther from civilization you are, the safer for you both."

Alarm bells exploded in Page's head. Not that she worried about leaving her friends. She didn't have any. Dad never allowed her to bring anybody home from school, and he didn't like to be friendly with neighbors. As for grandparents, she hardly knew Dad's folks. They traveled most of the year, living in their motor home. Dad said, "Good riddance! I don't need them around poking their noses in my business." Mom's parents had died when Page was a baby; she couldn't remember them. That left only Dad, Mom, and Page to be their family.

If she and Mom went thousands of miles away, then their family would be extinct. No way could she ever go home again, to the house surrounded by big shade trees, to her room with all the horse books she had collected and read till they were ragged. What would happen to Dad? Dad, Dad! Maybe it was her fault that things had gone wrong. If she weren't so big and clumsy, if she'd just listened instead of talking, if only she'd been more careful!

Page had burst into Lorna's kitchen shouting, "I'm not going to Panther Flat! I'll find me a place to stay—"

"Where?" Lorna flicked her cool eyes over Page. "Until your dad accepts help, he won't change. And until he changes, he's a walking time bomb." She slid papers across the breakfast table to Mom. "Fill out this application and we'll get it in the mail today."

"It's the only way," Mom said, catching Page's hand, almost pleading. "I have to take this job, if they'll have me."

Page whirled away from the two women and slammed out of the room.

By return mail, the president of the board of the Panther Flat school wrote that they wanted Mom immediately. Already it was the last week of August and school was set to begin in mid-September. The teacher's apartment was ready. The members of the board had been searching for their first "degree" teacher, the letter continued, and they were pleased to find someone qualified to teach not only science, which their students had never studied before, but the regular curriculum as well. Mom was so happy over the letter she read it aloud to Page, who pretended not to listen.

After that, events happened too fast for Page to make any sense of them. She distinctly remembered only two things: being outfitted with clothes from the shelves of donated garments in the welfare office's storeroom, and Lorna's refusal to drive past home on the way to the train station. Page had hoped to see their house, and maybe Dad, one more time.

"Don't look back," Lorna had warned. "It's your future that matters."

So they boarded the train, Page sulky and quarrelsome, Mom exhausted. Now they were deep into Texas, due to arrive at their destination about daylight.

Page blinked at the train window, shutting off her thoughts as deliberately as she would the TV at home. She turned to look at Mom. Ellie. She slept with her left hand relaxed in her lap. Page knew that a blank white band circled the ring finger where she'd worn her engagement diamond since Page could remember. The sparkling ring was gone, sold to buy the one-way train ticket for Page. The school board hadn't sent a ticket for the teacher's child. They didn't know she had one. "I can't tell them yet," Mom had said. "They might not hire me. Once we're there—somehow, we'll work it out."

Page sighed, her anger defused a little by the expression on her mother's face. Sleep erased the worry lines from her forehead, the tenseness from her mouth. She looked too young to be headed for a wilderness to teach at her first school, where she would be principal, classroom teacher, and janitor, according to her contract. Too young to face the school board with the news that she had in tow a clumsy twelve year old who, as Dad had said more than once, was deaf and dumb, had a hole in the head, and was just plain stupid—a bad bargain for anybody. The board would waste no time sending them away on the next train. Where could they go? They didn't belong anywhere. They didn't know anybody. What would they do? She could think of no answers to the questions crowding into her head. A weariness stole over her; her eyelids drooped. For a while she knew nothing until she heard her mother's excited voice, "Page! Wake up! We're here."

2

NUMB FROM LACK OF SLEEP, Page stood in the pre-
dawn darkness, watching the train disappear westward. No one was in sight except a man loading a cart
with boxes left by the train. As he rolled the freight
closer to where they huddled with their suitcases, he
seemed to size them up in one glance—bewildered,
cold, hungry.

"Come inside," he invited. The gray painted office
enclosed them in comforting brightness, shutting out
the morning twilight that seemed to conceal all kinds
of terrors, including Big Bend parents frowning over
an unexpected piece of baggage their new degree
teacher had brought.

"How far is Panther Flat?" Mom asked when the
man paused in his paperwork.

"Eighty miles south," he said without looking up.

Mom gasped. "Is there a bus? Or how do people get
there?"

"Well, on Fridays there's a bus. But today being
Monday, the only way to go there is with the mailman." He looked a question at them.

"I'm the new teacher," Mom explained.

He checked the big clock hanging on the gray wall

above a calendar. "The mailman isn't in town yet. We have time to go across the arroyo for a cup of coffee. After that, I'll get in touch with him." He sorted papers and stacked them, leaving the desk neat. Then he took a wide brim hat from a nail sticking out of a rough beam. "Your baggage can stay here." Leaving the door unlocked, he led them down into a ditch, then up and across a paved highway. He wore high-heeled cowboy boots and jeans, and moved through the cactus thorns and over the rocks in an easy lope.

In the pale light, Page saw one-story frame buildings lining the road. The town spread low into the distance, overlaid by the immense sky that seemed to press everything flat. A few buildings reared up false fronts in an effort, Page thought, to look more important, but they were still dwarfed by the vast sky that was slowly turning a lustrous pearl color.

The cafe slouched on the corner; two battered pickups were parked at careless angles to the curb in front. Inside, the place seemed crowded to Page though she saw only three people. Two men sitting at the counter, holding onto coffee cups, carried on a shouted conversation about football through the kitchen door with someone clattering skillets and pans out of sight. Like the depot man, they wore sombreros, jeans, and scuffed boots. Without pausing, they nodded a greeting. The juke box groaned out a country western at top volume. Gyrating around the box, and occasionally dipping a bow to it in order to stuff in a coin or poke a button, was what Page recognized as a high school football tackle. She thought of Dad, a football fanatic; though his daughter would never make the school team, he often said he would see to it that she was a football fan. He never let her miss a Saturday night game.

They seated themselves at a table by the window, Page teetering on the edge of her chair with the feeling she might have to leave in a hurry. The cook burst out of the kitchen, slamming two loaded plates onto the counter in front of the men, and refilling their coffee cups in one sweep.

By then the jukebox player had noticed the newcomers. He advanced upon their table, head thrust forward like a bulldozer clearing the way, and hands tugging at the sack apron wrapped round his middle.

"Jame," he acknowledged the depot man.

"Coffee," Jame said, and looked at Mom.

"For me too," Mom said. "But she'll have— pancakes?" She raised her eyebrows at Page, who clutched the table edge remembering how little money they had left from buying her ticket. She closed her mind against the thought and nodded yes.

Though the cook was now in the same room with the rest of them, he and the other customers still shouted at each other. While the burly waiter brought coffee for Mom and Jame, one of the men finished his breakfast, and clomped to the cash register. After ringing up the check, the cook gave him a farewell wallop that staggered him through the door. Then the waiter and the cook disappeared in back. On and on, the jukebox cried out the same sorrowful tune. Mom watched the action with big solemn eyes, probably wondering if her school kids would be this rambunctious.

Jame inspected Page over his steaming coffee. "Is she sick?"

"She didn't want to come," Mom explained.

"Not come? To the Big Bend?" Jame's voice rose in disbelief. "You'll never be the same after you've lived in the Big Bend."

Maybe that's the problem, thought Page. I don't want to change; I want to stay the same.

"Bloody Bend," Jame continued, his stormy gray eyes fixed on Page. "Some call it *el despoblado,* uninhabited land, but that's not true. Outlaws, bandits, smugglers, treasure hunters, maybe still some Comanches, are all hiding out down there, and I'd be right with them if. . . ." He paused, searching for words or maybe wondering if he'd said too much. "There're parts of the Big Bend where even now in 1953 a Texas Ranger won't go alone. *Nobody* should go alone." He glanced at his watch, scraped his chair back from the table and rose. "I'll send your baggage to the post office, and let the mailman know to expect you."

"Thank you," Mom said.

"You'll have time to go to the grocery store to pick up some grub. After you leave town there're no stores." He gave them directions.

"What does the mailman charge to ride with him?"

"A dollar each," Jame said.

Mom frowned. Page knew she was trying to figure how she could stretch their money to include transportation and groceries too. Page was too hungry to think of pinching pennies now. Maybe later, but not now. The big waiter clomped in with three pancakes and a jug of syrup. She wasted no time drowning the pancakes in golden syrup, and had two of them eaten before Jame disappeared into the arroyo.

She glanced up to ask a question and caught an expression on her mother's face that melted her stubborn anger for the moment. Slowly, she wiped her sticky mouth with a paper napkin, took a drink of water, and shoved the plate away.

"Here," she said gruffly, "I'm filled up."

Mom protested, but Page noticed she didn't waste any time starting to eat the pancake. "Mmmmmm," she said, scraping up every drop of syrup with her fork, and draining her coffee cup.

They went out into a brighter world. The sun was up, they had eaten, and Jame was taking care of getting them to Panther Flat. Mom counted over the bills remaining in her purse while they walked to the grocery store, a block off the main street.

"Beans and bread, and what else should we buy?" she asked.

Page didn't answer. She remembered self-righteously that Mom was the one who'd gotten them into this dry ugly town at the end of nowhere with hardly any money. She should be the one to get them out.

An olive-skinned, black-eyed boy, older than Page, was sweeping the narrow store aisle. She tensed at the sight of all the stuff crowding around her, knowing for sure that she would knock over something no matter how carefully she moved. This grocery store in no way resembled any supermarket she had ever seen. The dim light made it hard for Page to see, but one thing she couldn't miss was a large white cat with calm amber eyes watching her from the top of a stack of boxes.

Nearby, the grocer worked rapidly, checking through the apples, discarding one now and then. He looked as if he'd just gotten out of bed and come to work without a glance in the mirror.

Mom introduced herself and explained what she needed—food to take to Panther Flat to last them indefinitely. He gave her his immediate attention. "Oh, I heard you were coming," he said, eyeing Page without comment. "You don't have to worry, Mrs. Williams. Buy whatever you want and I'll charge it till the end of the month. Every Sunday I come to Panther Flat with a load of groceries. Just send me a list of what you need in Wednesday's mail and I'll bring it to you."

Relief lightened Mom's face.

"If you're going down with Jack Spencer today," the man continued, "I'd recommend taking just enough to get by till Sunday. He won't have much room, what with all the mail he hauls, and you two passengers." He proceeded to help Mom shop, chatting as they moved about the store.

Page lingered near the cat, wanting to pat it but not sure if she should. She had never had pets. Dad said that a cat was a nuisance, and a dog barked too much. She felt a hope stirring in her heart now, as she and the cat stared at each other. Maybe in Panther Flat she could have a kitten.

"Her name's Carlotta," the grocer called over his shoulder. "She likes to be petted."

Page reached out timidly. Carlotta seemed to smile and leaned forward to meet her hand, making a low trilling sound in her throat. What soft clean fur she had!

"Cleofas, watch the post office," the grocer told the boy. "Holler when you see the mailman coming."

"Sí," Cleofas said, going outside to sweep the sidewalk and watch.

By the time Cleofas called to them, Page had Carlotta in her arms, with Carlotta's paws kneading her neck. Smiling into the cat's amber eyes, Page felt a rush of gladness that seemed strange after such a long unhappy time. Carlotta looked back at her earnestly, as if she knew a secret she would tell Page if she could speak.

The grocer, who told them his name was Billy Newhouse, packed their purchases in a compact box which Cleofas carried out to the curb just as the mail van pulled in.

"Remember," Mr. Newhouse called, "send your list on Wednesdays. Anything else you need for the school, let me know."

3

THE MAILMAN, dressed the same as Jame and the men in the cafe, was wedged in with mailbags and packages, his long frame jackknifed under the wheel. Mom squeezed in front with him, while Page had to climb in back and make a place for herself. Even before they left town, the dusty van rattled and bucked as if it didn't want to go. Page braced herself for what she suspected would be the worst ride of her life. A hot wind whipped in through the lowered windows, snatching at her hair. The world was heating up, and the farther they drove south the more intense the heat became and the sparser the vegetation.

Jack Spencer said, "Panther Flat told me you'd be coming sometime this week, but they didn't mention the girl."

"No," said Mom.

Page squirmed, her cheeks burning. Before she could make an angry retort, a scrabbling sound in the floor distracted her. A snake! she thought, jerking her feet up with a muffled exclamation.

Mr. Spencer looked at her in the dusty mirror above his head. Over the noise of the car she heard him say, "Don't be afraid. It's only Domingo." Page held her breath, staring down where her feet had been. Gradually into view came tiny paws, then a small head and body. A trembling, pop-eyed dog looked up at her. Remembering how Carlotta liked being petted, Page lifted the little creature into her lap, feeling its rapid heartbeat, and stroking its ears that were flat-tened with anxiety. She talked soft and low, and the dog hid its face in her jacket.

"What does Domingo mean?" Mom asked.

"'Sunday' in Spanish. Domingo was born on a Sunday."

Page raised her voice so the mailman could hear. "Is Domingo afraid?"

"Yes," Mr. Spencer said. "Ever since my wife ran off and left us, he's been afraid."

"Oh, I'm sorry," Mom said.

"It's all right now." He turned to look at Mom, and said, like announcing a verdict, "Not everybody can take this Big Bend country."

Page hugged Domingo tighter, and stared out the window.

"We have a saying down here," the mail carrier continued, laughing, "that when God finished making the rest of the world he dumped the leftovers in the Big Bend."

Page believed that story. Wherever she turned she saw great piles of rocks. Boulders spilled across the dried ground so close together nothing but leafless plants could grow. The vast sky, now a burning blue, pressed down relentlessly, trying to keep her from breathing.

Ahead of them a tower of whirling dust rose up, like a savage giant fighting an invisible opponent. Then another one sprang up not far away, and another one, till as far as she could see whirlwinds moved among the stickers and the stones, each involved in an eerie private dance that was also part of an enormous overall dance involving hundreds of dust columns, rising and falling, expanding and contracting, moving near, moving far.

"Devil's witches," Jack Spencer said. "Count 'em."

Page tried. She reached fifty, counting by groups of five, but they changed too fast. New ones rose up for no reason, and old ones subsided into quiet dust.

She'd start counting again, but the erratic dancing, the disappearing and reappearing, confused her.

"They're always here no matter the season, no matter the time of day," he said. "Everything's still when you come on the scene. Then one rises up and starts dancing. That gets the rest of 'em going and they multiply by the dozens."

Page looked back to see if the devil's witches settled down after the van passed, waiting to put on another show for the next car that came along. Stacked up bags and boxes kept her from seeing. Could the dancing witches be a warning to keep out of the Big Bend?

She began noticing colors in the bluffs, tan and deep pink and lavender. The few plants that grew among the boulders bristled with long thorns. Away in the distance loomed barren mountains jagged as dinosaur teeth. Every few miles the van swooped down into what looked like a gully.

"Dry creek," Mr. Spencer said. *"Muy peligroso.* Never camp or picnic in one. The sky can be as clear as it is right now, but somewhere in the mountains rain may be falling—a Texas-size rain, torrential. It'll flood the dry stream bed, eight or ten feet deep. You wouldn't have a chance."

"Is that why the measuring stick is there?" Mom asked. "To show how deep the water is?"

"Yes, but even if the water measures only a foot or two deep, it's treacherous. I've seen boulders bigger than this van rolling toward the Rio Grande. It's not safe to mess with these dry creeks."

Along the way, Page saw several elongated piles of

rocks marked with weathered wooden crosses. Graves! On the bank of a dry creek she sighted two of them, one adult and one child size. No house was nearby, not even the ruins of a house, only the awful desert, and those looming mountains. How did they die in this lonely place?

When they went through a break in the mountain range, Jack Spencer said, "Here's Persimmon Gap. See those mountains way ahead? The Chisos—the Ghost Mountains. That's where your school is."

Page fastened her eyes on the hazy cluster of mountains. She had never seen real mountains before coming here. The brutal roughness of those they left behind them made her want to hide with Domingo. But the haunted ones in the distance ahead were strangest of all. They looked as if they were floating, with no connection to the earth.

"Ghost Mountains? Who haunts them?" she asked.

"An Apache chief, Alsate. You'll see him."

How could he say such a thing? Was Alsate a ghost anyone could see? She had looked at so much her eyes felt blistered. Her nose was chock-full of dust. As they jolted nearer the Chisos, she realized she would soon have to part from Domingo. To keep her eyes from seeing the Big Bend, she busied herself making a hiding place for him. By the time she finished, they had reached Panther Flat. Just ahead, almost hidden by bushes, were several inconspicuous houses. Farther on, off to itself across one of those arroyos like the one at the depot, sat a low cement block building with a wall of windows facing them.

"The school," Mr. Spencer said.

The road curved around and pulled up short at the back door where they parked. Here Page saw new swings and climbing bars, and space for ball games. Already the sun was lowering over the Chisos, which appeared to be just back of the playground. Page helped Domingo into his snug shelter, and crawled out to stand uncertainly on the rocky ground.

Mr. Spencer carried the groceries. Page and Mom, with a suitcase each, followed him through a large room equipped with new desks and stacked with boxes labeled in big letters "BOOKS." One long wall was floor-to-ceiling windows overlooking the mountains they had come through from town, range behind range, some smoky blue, some striped, some deep rose. Page had never seen a school like this one. Back home, teachers didn't want kids looking out the windows. Here, you couldn't help looking out.

A door from the schoolroom opened into a small apartment, one room with a bath. The hide-a-bed sofa, a breakfast table with two benches, a floor lamp beside an overstuffed chair, and a chest of drawers didn't leave much space. Outside the glass front door Page saw a cement patio.

"It's small," Mr. Spencer said doubtfully.

"We'll manage," Mom assured him.

"Let me know if I can do anything," he said, setting the box on the table.

"You've been a great help already," Mom said.

"I bring the mail three days a week, to the post office higher up in the mountains. The president of the board will probably be over there today. He's chief ranger for the park, y'know. Want me to tell him you're here?"

Mom thought a moment. "Yes, but will you please not mention my daughter? I've got to think how to break the news."

"Sure thing." He winked at Page. "Don't forget what they say—everything in the Big Bend country stings, sticks, or stinks. Be careful." And out he went.

Page ran after him to ask a question Mom must not hear. "What treasure do people hunt for?"

"Spanish treasure—a lost silver mine, a cave full of gold—take your choice." He waved a hand toward the mountains. "All in the Chisos, guarded by Alsate and an assortment of ghosts."

"Devil's witches too?"

"Maybe. Beware of treasure fever. It's highly contagious." He shifted gears, causing the van to shudder like a horse impatient to be off. "Treasure fever makes you do foolish and dangerous things." His tan face crinkled into a grin. "Domingo and I will check on you now and then. *Adios.*" He waved and roared away, spraying gravel.

Page watched the van disappear, followed by a roiling trail of dust, but her thoughts were in Alabama. Dad had caught treasure fever. He and Mom quarreled repeatedly over the time and money he spent looking for buried treasure. In his personal closet he kept "the finest metal detector available on the market" and all the accessories. Occasionally, he allowed Page to come with him to search DeSoto's campground from the

1540s or to follow a federal army trail of 1865. Once at an abandoned Confederate cemetery, in a pile of loose dirt he had dug, he found a chunk that made him throw down the sifting screen in excitement. "Pay dirt, Page!" he exclaimed, crumbling away the clay to a metallic core. "A uniform button, or I'm a monkey's uncle!"

He strode to the nearby stream, its clear water rushing over a bed of pebbles, and began scrubbing the button. In her eagerness to see, Page jarred his elbow. The shiny disk spun out of his palm and landed in the hurrying stream among a million small stones, disappearing instantly.

They searched until sundown, Dad passing from hot rage and cursing to cold rage and silence. Shut up together in the car on the way home after dark, Page apologized over and over, finally giving in to despairing sobs she couldn't control. That angered him more.

"If you don't shut up, I'll smash head-on into that next car. In fact, I will anyway." And he flicked his headlights on bright to blind the other driver, and shoved the accelerator so suddenly the car hiccuped, then shot ahead at a slant across the center line. Paralyzed with fear, Page choked back her crying. Whenever he'd made this threat before, he'd swerved at the last minute missing the other car by inches, and laughing about the fright he'd given the driver. Maybe he would swerve this time. Maybe he wouldn't.

"Page," Mom's voice brought her back to the warm sunshine and the mountains that concealed treasures of silver and gold. If she could discover a treasure! Dad would be proud of her then. He might even love her. No, he could never love her—she was too big and awkward and dumb—but if she could only make him proud, that would be enough. She wiped her eyes with the back of her hand and went inside the school.

4

THE PRESIDENT OF THE BOARD didn't appear for a couple of hours, time enough to put away the groceries and unpack their suitcases. Page changed into wrinkled shorts and flip-flops. She was sprawling on the sofa where she couldn't see the out-of-doors when she heard his car tires crunching the gravel back of the school, then the sound of the outside door opening.

"Mrs. Williams?" a man's voice called.

Page quietly shut herself in the bathroom. She heard her mother greeting him, and listened to their voices, but she couldn't understand their words. Too soon, Mom called her to come out, and she had to face Mr. Allman.

He was muscular, not fat, and wore a park service uniform of olive green. On the table lay his stiff-brimmed Stetson hat. His furrowed face had a dimple in the chin, and he studied her with unwavering brown eyes.

"I'm surprised," he said. "We're not prepared for her." He glanced around the small apartment.

Page said nothing.

"We'll manage," Mom said, as if reassuring herself.

With a thoughtful expression he gazed toward the

distant mountains. Then he cleared his throat. "I'll have to discuss this with the board." He looked at Page again. "It's just that I'm surprised," he repeated. He picked up his hat, turning it round and round in his brown hands.

"I know," Mom murmured. "I'm sorry."

He nodded and changed the subject. "Opening day is Monday. Sixteen pupils are enrolled, grades one through seven. Some of your students are children of park employees. One is from Mexico. You'll have two from ranches outside the park." An undecided look came over his face. "One of your first graders is a cowhand on a ranch beyond the Dead Horse Mountains." He tilted his head toward the blue range half-filling the eastern sky. "He'll drive another ranch child to school, eighty-six miles round trip. That is, if he can pass his driver's test. He's the best ranch hand around, but he doesn't know how to drive."

Now it was Mom's turn to nod. Page thought she looked dazed.

"The board will meet with you soon to go over everything," Mr. Allman continued, "and discuss what's to be done about—er—your daughter. For now, I'm due over at the park headquarters." He pointed to a long low building to the right across another arroyo, then he gestured to the left at the group of houses. "In case you need anything, I live in that second house. We don't have phones so just walk on over." He settled his hat on his head and with another little nod, left through the schoolroom. They heard the outside door shut.

Mom sank into the overstuffed chair. "What did he

say? A first grader driving? A cowboy! Whatever will I do?"

Page was seized with a powerful desire to laugh, not ha-ha laughing, but loud crazy laughing. She controlled herself by holding her nose till she got the bathroom door shut again. Then she sat on the edge of the tub, laughing and crying into a towel to keep Mom from hearing. Those noisy people in the cafe, the dancing devil's witches, dry creeks that drown you, haunted mountains with no trees, and a cowboy in the first grade—what a weird place!

When Page finally came out, Mom was rummaging through the cupboards above the stove. "All the equipment we need is here. Look at this refrigerator." She pressed a button to the right of the stove, and a door opened to reveal empty white shelves. Page knew from her red-rimmed eyes that Mom had been crying too.

"What's that motor that runs all the time?" Page asked.

"A generator, behind one of these hills. He said it makes electricity for Panther Flat. Did you hear him say no phones? And no television either."

Page stared at her. No phones didn't faze her—she had nobody to call—but no TV? What did the kids do after school? Then she remembered—after the board meeting, she and Mom might not be living here anyway.

They'd each occupied themselves with getting settled in when footsteps rattled the stones along the path to their front door. A girl in jeans and sturdy shoes appeared carrying a tray covered with a white cloth. "My mom sent your supper," she said. Page smelled odors that made her mouth water as Mom took the tray. The girl was tall, with hair and eyes the same shade of tawny brown. "I'm Allis Lawrence. Allis with an 's.' That's my house, the nearest one over there. I'm in seventh grade." She paused to catch her breath.

"I'm Page and I'm in sixth." She could hardly shape the words without stammering she felt so nervous. Here was someone who might become her friend if only she, Page, didn't blunder. I will be oh so careful, she promised herself, and took a deep breath.

"Can you come out?" Allis asked. Page nodded and followed her. They sat on the edge of the cement patio which held the warmth of the sun. "The other kids are crazy to see the new teacher. Their moms won't let them worry you this first day." Allis smiled around her braces. "I'm glad I got to bring your supper."

Allis did most of the talking at first. Page couldn't loosen her tongue to say more than "Yes," or "Ummm," or "No." While they talked, the shadows lengthened and the mountain ranges changed to brilliant colors that reflected a brightness on all the world. Allis named the mountains, starting to their left beyond the quiet houses and moving to the right. "Lone Mountain—we climb that a lot. Way off is Santiago with the flat top. Dog Canyon's that way—lots of caves there. The Dead Horse Mountains are the stretched-out blue ones. The Rosillas are red, the Sierra del Carmens striped—they're in Mexico."

"Is Mexico so near?" Page asked, forgetting her shyness.

"Near, but not that near. Everything looks closer than it really is," Allis said.

Page felt overwhelmed by the enormous space that dwarfed the buildings across the arroyo, and made humans seem insignificant. She brought their conversation around to familiar things. "Do you have a pet? I'm going to get a dog or a cat."

Allis's eyes widened. "You can't have a pet in a national park."

"What do you mean?"

"You can't have anything that upsets the balance of nature. The only animals here are wild ones."

"What kind?"

"All sorts—coyotes, foxes, bobcats, panthers."

Page stood up, aghast. "You mean coyotes and bobcats and—uh—panthers run loose here?" Immediately she regretted her outburst, fearful that Allis would be offended.

But she answered calmly, "All around, everywhere. Black panthers, too, but rarely. I've never seen a black one."

That was too much for Page to take in. "Let's go swing."

Behind the school, they took turns pushing each other as high as the swing would go. Allis nodded toward the Chisos. "That mountain with the squeezed in top is even named Panther Peak."

"Have you seen a ghost?"

Allis hesitated for a millisecond. "I've seen Alsate, of course."

"Do you know about the treasure he guards?"

"Everybody knows about that treasure. It's gold

bars or gold nuggets. Nobody's sure which. Sometimes we go searching for it."

"Will you take me?" Page clenched her fists around the swing and held her breath waiting for the answer.

"Sure. There's a lost silver mine too. We've found the trail to it. But we always lose it." Allis stopped pushing her. "Let the cat die, then it's my turn."

As the swing slowed, gradually making shorter and shorter swoops, Page thought about the treasures. "Which would you rather find, the gold or the silver?"

"I think the gold," Allis said matter-of-factly. "It's already mined. And probably it's packed in chests if it's bars, or in goatskin pouches if it's nuggets."

They stared at the Chisos, as if the fortune were theirs for the taking.

Abruptly Allis brought them back to reality. "You only have boys in your grade—Epifanio from Dripping Springs, and Mack, a sick pill of a boy from a ranch on the river."

"Will Mack ride to school with that cowboy?"

"No, Mack lives closer to Cow Heaven than to the Dead Horse Mountains. His folks are mad because your mom was hired. They didn't want an outside teacher."

For a time the only sound was the creaking of the swing chains as Page pushed Allis higher and higher.

"What teacher did they want?" Page asked.

"The old one, only she's young. She was teacher at our other school, higher in the mountains. We had a rickety building that wouldn't heat. We nearly froze in the winter. And ringtails lived in the attic. Sometimes they played so loud we couldn't hear Mrs. Boatwright,"

Allis laughed. "The Boatwrights live over there. From here our house comes first, then the Allmans, then the Boatwrights."

Page repeated the names to herself, staring at the houses across the arroyo, hoping she would remember all that Allis was telling her. "I don't understand. Why are they mad?"

"Mrs. Boatwright expected to be in charge of the new school," Allis said, pumping the swing so high

her feet reached for the blue sky. Page thought she would surely arc over the top and complete a circle. "But the board wanted a teacher with a college degree, like your mom. The Boatwrights and their friends are really mad." Allis let the swing slow down, then leaped from it at a run.

"You didn't let the cat die," Page objected. "I'll race you to the back of the playground."

"You need better shoes," Allis frowned at Page's feet. "We've got snakes the color of the ground—you'll step on one. But you won't have any trouble seeing the green rattlers and the red racers. You need to wear jeans, too. If Mack shoves you in a cactus the way he did me last year, you'll get thorns big as needles that'll work their way through your legs and out the other side."

Page stared toward the edge of the playground, now in the shadow of the Chisos. Thorns! Snakes! Panthers! Ghosts! What else? Ringtails!

"What's a ringtail?"

"Sort of like a raccoon, but smaller. Big bushy tail with rings."

"Do panthers come around here?"

"Lots of times. Deer too. If you put out a water pan, all kinds of animals will come to drink."

"Let's do! Except panthers. I'd rather not have them."

"Wherever the deer are, the panthers are."

They searched through the bin left by the construction workers until they found an old hubcap shaped like a bowl.

"If this holds water, it'll do till you get a better one," Allis said.

They filled it at an outside faucet, then chose a spot a few feet from the patio at the base of a plant Allis called a Spanish dagger. They steadied the hubcap in a circle of rocks.

"Animals will come real close. You can even take pictures."

"Every night?"

"Probably. I'd better go now."

Page walked a short way with Allis along the road, but mindful of her flip-flops and the snakes, she soon turned back.

After supper, Mom disappeared into the school to work, and Page went out on the patio to watch for animals. She felt safe sitting against the wall near the apartment's front door in the shadows. Moonlight showed the bushes and rocks, and at the foot of the tall dagger plant she could see the water gleaming in the hubcap. Across the arroyo to the left were lights in those desert-colored houses where the president of the school board and Allis lived, and Mrs. Boatwright, the teacher Mom was replacing. The headquarters building, across the arroyo to the right, was dark now except for a couple of outside lights. The mountain ranges reared up black against the sky.

While watching and waiting, Page thought back over the day, her first in this forgotten pocket of the world. She couldn't count all the people she'd met since climbing down from the train. Well, she couldn't claim she'd met them exactly. She noticed most people here didn't introduce themselves. They seemed to take it for granted that you'd get to know who they were in good time, and that there wasn't any hurry.

Carlotta and Domingo—she could hardly wait to see the amber-eyed cat and the little dog again. And Allis. How could she know so much? She was like a nature book talking. Allis had searched for a lost silver mine in the Chisos. She had promised to take Page treasure hunting. Allis had seen Alsate, the Apache chief whom Jack Spencer predicted Page would see too. Did the ghost of Alsate truly guard the lost treasure? Were the mysterious devil's witches dancing tonight beyond those dark mountain ranges? Page shivered. Maybe she didn't want to sit out here in the dark watching for wild animals after all. If a panther should pad around the corner of the building, what would she do? A black panther would be invisible. Quickly, she rose and went inside.

By the time Mom came out of the schoolroom Page had the sofa unfolded and their bed made. After lights out, she remembered the intent look Carlotta gave her that morning. It seemed ages ago, but what she realized as she held Carlotta and looked in her beautiful eyes was still vivid—that being happy felt good, better than being angry. Suddenly, she wished she'd answered when Mom told her goodnight. "Mom," she called softly. Mom's relaxed, even breathing showed she was already asleep.

5

PAGE WAS OUT OF BED EARLY ENOUGH next morning to see the sun rise from behind the Dead Horse Mountains and start on its path across the sky to the Chisos. While Mom worked at her desk, Page unpacked boxes of old library books that had come from the former school.

Light poured through the window-wall that faced east, highlighting the titles as Page shelved them. She noticed they covered subjects such as hydrology, geology, theology, Texas history, Big Bend history, geography, sheep and goat raising, garlic growing, and cotton farming on the Rio Grande. For several minutes she examined a collection of Big Bend legends and treasure stories which she decided to set aside in a special place. She wanted to read that one first. Most of the books were ragged and out-of-date. Different names were scrawled inside the covers. It was as if they were castoffs from old home libraries.

A knock on the playground door startled Page. A boy stepped inside, dressed in jeans and a faded shirt, wearing sturdy high-top shoes. Wiry red curls escaped from the edge of the billed cap he wore and freckles splashed across his face.

"I'm Bret from over there." He nodded toward the houses across the arroyo. "Fifth grade. Want to go hiking?" He was talking to Page but looking at Mom. He had a canteen strapped on his hip.

"Fine with me," Mom said to Page, who wasn't sure she wanted to go. On second thought, why not?

"I'm almost finished. Can you wait a minute?"

"We'll help," Bret said. "Yo!" he yelled out the door. Another boy appeared, identical to Bret.

"I'm Bart," he said. "We're hiking to the Comanche camp." The boys didn't remove their caps or canteens, but worked with enthusiasm. In a short time the boxes were emptied and the books arranged according to subject matter.

The boys talked with Mom while Page hunted for her tennis shoes. She had chosen them in a hurry at the welfare supply room, and they were too big. Remembering why she didn't have her own shoes made her falter, but she set her jaw, and looked around for some kind of hat. There wasn't one, of course, so on the paper Mom taped to the refrigerator door, Page wrote "hat," then erased it and wrote "cap." Already Mom had written "sturdy shoes for P." That was the list for when Mom's first pay check came. The other growing list was for groceries to be mailed to Billy Newhouse on Wednesday, tomorrow.

Page tucked in her shirt and headed out. Bart and Bret, exactly alike, were telling Mom about their former teacher.

"She taught just ordinary things like reading and spelling and arithmetic."

"Yeah," said the other. "We never had science. She didn't know much."

Mom smiled. "If she knew how to teach all that, I'd say she knew quite a bit."

"She hates you," one of them said. "'Cause you got her job."

"And Mack Hill's folks are her friends. They hate you too," said the other cheerfully. "But we don't. We're glad you came."

"We want to learn about the universe and stuff," one said.

Page followed the twins toward the playground.

"You need a cap," one brother said.

"Where did you say you're going?" Mom called after them.

"Comanche Butte." The boys answered together and pointed toward the horizon.

"Be back before lunch," Mom said.

"Okay," the boys nodded.

They struck out southwestward, toward a point to the left of the Chisos. Before long Page discovered that wearing a hat in Big Bend was not just a fad. The sun burned hot! When they came up out of the arroyo, she couldn't see shade anywhere ahead, only scraggly, life-less bushes and occasionally taller plants bristling with knife-like leaves. Rounded cactus plants, barely showing out of the ground and thick with spines curving like fish hooks, made her uncomfortably aware of her flimsy shoes. Trying to avoid several of them growing close to-gether, Page floundered into a harmless-looking bush. In an instant the bush seemed to sprout vicious thorns that held her fast. The boys came back to free her.

"Catclaw," one of them said.

"They reach out and grab you," added the other.

The catclaw bush had ripped her shirt and left bloody scratches on her arms. The boys took no notice, but plodded toward a steep hill-like formation that stood at the far edge of the flat. Page's mouth felt parched.

Before reaching the butte, they took time out in the meager shade of several greenish-yellow bushes. Page touched her finger to her tongue, rubbed it on her nose, then inhaled deep in the bushes. Strong disinfectant odor filled her lungs.

"Creosote bush," one said. "What're you doing?"

"I'm trying to smell the way horses do. They smell lots of odors we don't. And they read them the way we read a map."

"Neat," one of them said. He wet the tip of his nose, too, and buried his face in the bushes. "It works," he said, looking at Page with interest.

The other one panted, "Water," and unscrewed his canteen. His brother did the same. They tilted their heads back with their eyes closed and let the water gurgle down their throats. Page swallowed hard and coughed.

One of them licked his lips. "Want a drink?"

She took the canteen out of his hands before he finished asking. The water was lukewarm, but still it soothed her dry and dusty throat. She sighed, handing it back.

"You need a canteen," he said.

These kids are all kind of bossy, Page thought. Allis had said, "You need better shoes," and, "You need jeans." Bart/Bret had said, "You need a cap," and, "You need a canteen."

"This is where Comanches camped on their way to Mexico," Bret/Bart said. "Apaches, too."

"Mescalero Apaches." The other boy rolled the words over his tongue.

"They made arrowheads here." He showed her shiny chippings, every color she knew and some she'd never imagined, scattered over the ground. Now that she was looking she saw them everywhere, like glistening particles of a shattered rainbow, brightening the dun colored ground.

"I want one of every color!" She scrambled to her feet, then hesitated. "Can I have them?"

"Yeah. Nobody comes here but us kids."

"Sometimes we find arrowheads." Now the boys were collecting too, handing her especially pretty chips.

"They aren't like the other rocks around here," she said.

"They're not from here. The different tribes brought them."

"From somewhere else. While they camped here they chipped away on arrowheads and tools."

"I found a hide scraper once."

The twins fitted their bits of information together like two people working the same jigsaw puzzle.

"Here's an agate." One of the brothers laid in her hand a sun-warmed wad of writhing gray worms, except that they were stone. "Bird guts," he said. Now Page could see that the agate looked like the entrails of a small creature that had met with an accident, even to the dark red streaks resembling blood. She had never seen a rock like it. Dad would surely think it odd. She had to keep it for him.

By now her pockets sagged with the weight, but she wanted more. How exciting to think that the last human to touch these chips was a real Comanche, or a Mescalero Apache. The boys soon got bored and started off again. Reluctantly Page followed.

Climbing the butte wasn't easy. The mealy ground slid from under her feet, moving her downward one step for each two she took upward. Then there were those ever-present rocks that showered down the incline every time she stirred. At the top she and the twins sat on a ledge and drank from the canteens again. She wanted to drink from the other boy's canteen this time to be fair, but she couldn't tell which one she'd drunk from before.

"How can I know which one is who?" she asked.

They laughed, their teeth showing white in their freckled faces.

"There's a way," one said.

"But we don't tell," the other said.

"That's for us to know and you to find out," they chanted together, then fell over laughing. They lay still, drowsing in the sun, their caps over their faces. Page relaxed against the lumpy butte, shading her eyes to see the awesome mountains surrounding the flat. She hardly recognized the Chisos, they looked so different from here.

"Are panthers really on Panther Peak?" She wanted to see if their answer would agree with what Allis had said.

"Sure," the redhead nearest her said.

"All over the Chisos," the other one added.

"Ghosts, too?"

"Yeah."

"Alsate?"

"Um-hum," one said.

"Not just Alsate," the other murmured. "Outlaws."

"Bandits."

"Silver mines."

"Lost treasure. We go on expeditions searching."

She said doubtfully, "Sounds like a made-up story to me. It's too much—Indians, outlaws, bandits, silver mines, lost treasure, ghosts."

"It's true," one of them said, rolling to his feet and yawning. "They're here."

She noticed that he spoke in the present.

The other one sat up, looking at her with his clear green eyes. "Everybody knows, and it's all in books."

"One more swig before we go," his brother said.

As Page turned up the warm metal canteen, she remembered that back home she had been very particular about drinking out of a clean glass. The "back home" Page would shudder to see how gladly she drained the canteen after these two boys she hardly knew.

"Deer," one of them pointed.

Page could make out the animals, even though they were at some distance and blended with the sandy beige color of boulders and ground. She counted four.

The boys started down, triggering a shower of rocks that clattered loud in the still, warm air. The deer, instantly alert, flipped up their white-flag tails and bounded out of sight. She laughed.

"White-tailed deer," one boy called up to her.

"Mule deer are here, too," the other said. "They've got big ears."

She watched the brush where the deer had been, remembering that panthers might be stalking them. She could see nothing but bushes, ground, and boulders, all the same lifeless color. She slipped and slid down the steep side of Comanche Butte.

On the way back to the school the boys showed her a grainy gray rock, worn down in the middle like a bowl. "A *metate*," one of them explained. "The Indians ground stuff, like mesquite beans, in it."

The other boy picked up a rock nearby that was the same gray color. It fit exactly in his hand. "A *mano*," and he demonstrated how the Indians used it to crush seeds in the metate. Page wanted to hold the *mano* too, thinking of the Apache or Comanche woman who last used it. She could feel the woman's presence at this old campground. No wonder people thought the Chisos were haunted.

They didn't talk much after that, except when the boys asked if she liked having her mother for her teacher. Page had been worrying about that very thing, but all she said was, "I don't know yet. She's never been my teacher before."

As they parted on the playground, one of them grinned at her impishly and said, "Which one am I?"

Page stared at him without speaking.

"You don't know, do you?" the other one chortled.

"Of course I do," she said haughtily.

"Which one? Which one?" They danced around her, yelling. "Bret? Bart?"

She refused to answer, and they went off toward home laughing. She determined she would learn the secret of how to tell them apart.

After lunch she spread the Indian chips on the cement patio.

"They feel so smooth and cool," Mom said, letting them pour through her fingers. "And what unusual colors." She suggested that when they finished eating the peanut butter, the chips would look pretty in the clear glass jar. They could set the jar in the window where the colors showed best, and look at them anytime.

6

WEDNESDAY MORNING as soon as Page had time she took the Big Bend legend book to the shade of the school porch facing the Chisos. She carefully leafed through the closely printed pages, brown and brittle with age. Just as she had hoped, treasure stories were included. Her heart beat faster to see that certain passages were marked, and notes scrawled beside some of the maps. The handwritings didn't match, so Page knew that more than one person had pored over this treasure manual.

She studied the pictures of the warriors. What strong faces they had: square jaws, high cheekbones, sharp eyes, long black hair. Every so often she glanced toward the mountains, thinking about the Comanches camping on the flat, making their way to and from Mexico. They always came in September, the small print said, and made their raids on the settlers across the Rio Grande when the moon came full. The Mexico Moon it was called. Page was deep in her imagining when Allis startled her with a cheerful, "Hi! Have you done your Billy list?" She held several letters in her hand.

Page struggled to bring her mind back to the porch and her friend. Wednesday. Billy list? Yes, the grocery list for Billy Newhouse.

She scrambled to her feet. "I'll get it. Look at these old stories. Think they're true?"

When Page returned with the list, folded into a stamped, addressed envelope, Allis said, "I've heard lots of these, some of them a little different. The Spanish silver mine up in the Chisos—that's the one we've tried to find."

"Is it true about the cholera?"

"Maybe. I heard that the Spaniards made slaves of the Indians. They forced them to work the silver mine up there." She nodded toward the Chisos. "They stayed on the river at San Vicente where the chapel is now. The trail they used to go to the mine is the one we've followed."

"Wow!"

"But it's too long ago," Allis sighed. "Yes, cholera killed everybody except the Indian guard at the mine. He lived on in a cave, nobody knows how long. He's one of the ghosts in the Chisos."

"ONE of the ghosts?"

"Yes. There's Alsate, and lots of others." She laid the book down. "Sometimes at night I look this way and see lights moving about." She shuddered, but a laugh twinkled in her eyes as she added, "Now that you're here, the ghost will get you instead of crossing the arroyo for me."

"Be serious," Page insisted. "Do you truly see lights in the Chisos?"

"Yes. And I'm not the only one." She paused. "Let's take the lists to the mailbox before Mr. Spencer comes."

"What if we missed the mail? We'd go hungry, wouldn't we?"

"No. Billy would pack a box of food anyway—things he thought you needed. He makes sure nobody goes without."

The mailbox stood in a network of cactus plants where the Panther Flat road joined the main road.

"To the left, and up, is the lodge where tourists stay, and the post office and souvenir shop. Kathy and her sister Mary live up there. Right, and down, goes to Margaret's on the river."

"A long way, isn't it?" Page asked.

"Yes. In both directions. Straight ahead to town is longer yet."

Looking that way, they saw dust churning along the road like tan smoke.

"That's Mr. Spencer now," Allis guessed.

"Let's wait for him," Page suggested, thinking of Domingo.

In the meantime they inspected a bird nest attached horizontally to the thorny cactus branches that were like green chains woven together.

"A cactus wren's." Allis shut one eye to peer inside the tunnel-like entrance. "Nobody's in it this late in the year."

"It's as long as a loaf of bread," Page marveled. "And built to stay—it's like a part of the cactus." How could a creature small as a bird, or maybe a pair of birds, weave such an outsized, intricate nest?

"The basket-making Indians who used to live here learned to weave from watching the birds, I've heard," Allis said.

Page thought that over. "Are they different from Comanches and Apaches?"

"Very different—more peaceful, not wanderers. They're called cave dwellers, too."

The dusty old van pulled up beside the mailbox. "I've got a parcel of books for the teacher," Jack Spencer greeted them. "Want a ride over?"

They hopped in, looking for Domingo, but he didn't come out of hiding till they parked at the school. While Mr. Spencer drank a cup of coffee with Mom, the girls coaxed Domingo to play on the cool cement floor of the schoolroom.

"We need a ball," Allis said, looking around. Suddenly she kicked off her shoes, removed her cotton socks and rolled them together to make a soft, soundless ball. On all fours, they taught Domingo to chase it, and to run with it while they chased him. He soon lost his timidity and played with enthusiasm, barking now and then in his excitement.

"It's good to hear him bark," Jack Spencer said. "He hasn't been that happy in a long time. But we have appointments to keep. Got to go."

They made him promise a return visit, and both of them carried the little dog, half-and-half, to the van. They watched it out of sight, then went to help unpack the box, which contained new books with bright covers and many pictures. The books' spines creaked when they were opened, and they smelled of printers' ink and fresh paper.

Page wet her nose and bent close to smell them better. "I love new books!" she declared. "But maybe old ones are more interesting, when you think about all the people who've read them." She was remembering the Big Bend legends, and the notations made by the different readers.

Later she and Allis looked through the old book, studying the maps, and trying to decipher some of the handwriting. Allis had the exciting idea that some of the hard-to-read notes were written in code, but until they got a magnifying glass they couldn't be sure. At noon when Allis left, Page watched her go along the curving road toward home. She felt a happiness that was strange to her, but she knew what it was—the happiness of having a friend.

Mr. Allman arranged to take Mom to a school board meeting up in the mountains on Wednesday night. While she waited for him, Mom fidgeted around the apartment, changing her blouse and redoing her hair. She said she didn't want supper. Page felt nervous too, because one of the things the board would decide was what to do about her. These three days in the Big Bend hadn't completely won her over, but life here was wonderful in one way—the peacefulness that she and Mom had for the first time that Page could remember. They had their disagreements, but they no longer feared the constant threat of Dad's temper explosions which had kept Page so anxious that she always said or did the wrong thing.

Yet, at this distance and in this peace, she loved Dad more than ever. She thought of him in the mornings before she slid out of bed. She thought about him at night, last thing before falling asleep. It was like saying goodnight to him, something she never dared do at home, for fear of reminding him of some blunder she'd made that day. Then he would rant for hours about Page's faults and mistakes. Page felt disloyal to Dad for hoping that tonight the board would be willing to let her stay in the Big Bend at least long enough for her and Allis to locate the lost Chisos treasure. Page was sure that even if they found only a small part of it—say one or two gold bars—everything wrong in her life would be set right.

7

AS SOON AS MOM LEFT WITH MR. ALLMAN, Page
assembled a supper from leftovers in the refrigerator. She took the plate out onto the patio so she could
watch the hubcap as dark came on. Every morning she
had to add water, but she could never see what was
drinking it. The rocks around the hubcap showed no
footprints to give her a clue.

She settled herself on the edge of the cement slab,
bare feet firmly on the ground, balancing the plate on
her knees. She was glad that the deepening twilight
kept her from seeing the food clearly. Allis's dad had
gone dove hunting in Mexico, and Allis brought over
a platter of the birds nestled in some kind of greens.
They looked like a picture in a cookbook, but Page
recoiled from the sight of the plump little bodies.

"They're game birds," Allis said. "Eating is what
they're for, and are they ever good!"

And they were, as Page found out. However, she
still felt more comfortable not thinking of what they
used to be.

Now she gnawed the tasty bones clean, and piled
them on the ground beside her feet until she could
dump them in the garbage. Watching the transition
from day to night in this vast lonely country absorbed

her attention. Lights came on in the houses across the arroyo, but at this distance she could see no one moving about. She could see no animals approaching the water either, though she knew they might be all around her.

She added the last bone to the discards and began eating the fruit salad and a roll. Sniffing and sneezing sounded around the corner of the house, approaching fast. She froze. A skunk, about the size of a cat, hurried into sight, looking neither right nor left but coming straight toward Page. She could see it well because its body was blacker than the night, and a wide white band down the middle of its back shone like a neon light. The long fluffy tail trailed behind. The animal did not pause in its path to Page's feet. Her first thought was to dump the plate and flee, but her body was paralyzed. She didn't move. It was a good thing, too. She might have startled the skunk and gotten sprayed—a disaster, according to Allis. "You stink forever," she'd said. "It makes you sick to your stomach. You can go blind, and become unconscious. I know lots of people who've been squirted."

These warnings ran through Page's mind while she watched the skunk come at her. Surely, when the skunk realized she was a person, it would run away. She held onto that hope, but the skunk dived into the pile of dove bones, crunching them like a cat. Around the corner came another skunk, twice as big as the first one. It rippled toward her, and shouldered the smaller one away. The small one growled fiercely and raised its tail, ready to fire. The larger skunk didn't falter, but took sole possession of the bones, cracking them expertly. The small one danced around, tail raised high, stamping its front feet and fussing like an angry cat. The second one raised its beautiful tail in warning, and growled. Crack, crunch, crack, went the bones.

Now from around the corner appeared the grandest skunk of all, broad and plump, with such a wide white

stripe down its back that almost no black showed. Like a royal personage, it undulated to the dove bones. The second skunk gave way, but with furious protests. All three milled around Page's bare feet, growling, meowing, fussing, and foot-stamping. Page tried to shrink her feet by making toe fists, scrunching her toes as tight underfoot as possible. That's when the little one, stamping around the two big ones who were scuffling, touched its nose to her foot. That cool black nose electrified Page with visions of long sharp teeth that crunched dove bones as if they were dry twigs. She reacted in terror—her tight toes uncoiled like a spring, striking the skunk in the face. The skunk leaped straight up; all of them retreated with raised tails and growling threats. Page braced herself. She expected to be sprayed not by one skunk but three. Mom would come home to find her unconscious, blinded, and reeking of skunk stench.

No! If she were going to get sprayed, she would at least try to save herself. Very slowly she groped for the bones that were left on the ground. Slowly, in a nonthreatening way, she tossed them to the animals. They watched her every move, tails still poised tall. Slowly, she tore the roll in chunks which she tossed after the bones. That caught their attention. With the food widely scattered, each skunk ate without interference, ignoring Page.

She crept inside as quietly as possible, putting the plate in the sink. She couldn't think of eating another bite or cleaning the kitchen. She threw herself on the sofa and lay in the dark, trembling. She even sobbed a little. Her escape had been so narrow! Finally, she got up to take a shower. That seemed to wash away the imagined skunk spray, and helped her back to feeling normal.

By the time Mom came home, Page was much calmer. She described how beautiful the skunks were, and how much like cats they acted, and why she was afraid. Mom hugged her and said she had acted with good judgment. Then she asked, "Did you learn anything from this adventure?"

Page thought for a while. Then she said slowly, "Wild animals are WILD animals. They aren't pets."

"I'm glad you know that," Mom said.

While they carried out their nightly routine of transforming the sitting area into their bedroom, Mom told Page about the board meeting. "They want us to stay," she said, sounding pleased. "But they are concerned that the apartment's too small for the two of us. They think you may get bored living at school, and that you might cause problems."

"I'll try not to cause problems," Page answered, and she meant it.

"More than worry over you, though, is their concern about keeping the peace. The community's been torn apart over hiring an outside teacher. The board asked me to be careful not to say or do anything that will antagonize anybody. They didn't name names, but I believe it's the Boatwrights and the Hills who may make trouble. I'm wondering where the twins' parents stand in this situation."

Page had wondered, too, but she didn't know what to say except to repeat, "I'll try not to make trouble."

8

MOM OFFERED PAGE A JOB as school janitor. At first Page said, "No, thanks!" because scrubbing bathrooms and sweeping and mopping didn't appeal to her. But then Mom added, "You could earn money to replace the horse books you had to leave behind."

After thinking it over, Page decided the job was a good idea. She wrote out a contract specifying what she would do and what pay she would receive. Mom read it carefully.

"It's good you've listed your jobs—scrub the sinks, clean and disinfect the toilets, mop the bathroom floors, polish the mirrors, empty the trash, sweep the schoolroom. But shouldn't you say something about when you'll get these chores done—as soon as school is out for the day, or by supper time, or first thing in the morning before school opens?"

"Maybe as soon as school is out would be best, before I unwind." Page wrote it into the contract.

"Another thing," Mom said, "how about agreeing that I won't have to remind you more than once about getting the work done?"

"Maybe twice."

"Once," Mom said firmly. "After all, you'll have it spelled out in the contract, too."

Page yielded. They made a few other adjustments, then she copied over the contract with hardly any cross outs. After they had both signed it, Page put it away in her bureau drawer with such a glow of satisfaction she was inspired to inventory the cleaning equipment and supplies at once.

That's where she was, in the supply closet that opened onto the playground, when she heard horse hooves. Heart hammering, she dropped everything and stepped outside. A boy she hadn't seen before was leading a bright chestnut horse toward the school, a big chestnut, with no other mark besides a star on his forehead. But he wasn't happy about being here. He kept jerking back, and flinging his head to one side so that the boy had to hold tight to the reins wrapped around his hands.

"What's the matter?" Page kept her voice low.

"I dunno. He must smell a mountain lion or something."

The horse blared his eyes at Page and snorted so hard he sprayed her with spit. He rolled one eye toward her, and the other eye backward to the boy. Page stood still as a post, watching him.

She remembered reading in one of her books at home about befriending a horse. She had never had a chance to practice it because she'd not been close to a horse before. She breathed deeply of his distinctive smell, a mix of horse sweat, old leather, and dust. The horse threw up his head and stiffened his front legs.

"What's his name?" she asked in the same quiet
voice.

"Victorio," the boy said.

Still not moving, she repeated the name softly,
putting into the word all the yearning she felt to be his
friend. The horse flicked his slender ears toward her,
and returned her intent look with a spark of interest

in his eyes. He took a halting step toward her, and stopped. When Page didn't move he stretched his nose, almost touching her, and smelled. She could hardly keep from reaching her hand out, but that wasn't the next step as she remembered it. When he seemed satisfied with the way she smelled, she saw the wildness fade from his eyes. Now, she knew, was the moment. Slowly, she bent toward him, speaking his name, until her face was almost against his and their breathing mingled. His breath smelled like sweet grass. She hoped hers was as pleasant to him. They stood so for a minute, then Page straightened, and offered her hand to him, every movement in slow motion. All the while, she talked softly, using his name. Don't show fear, don't even think fear, she remembered. Victorio allowed her to stroke his face, then, as she eased closer, his jaw and his neck. The boy grinned, watching them.

"He likes you," he said, relaxing a little.

"Can I hold him?" she asked. "My mom's inside if you want to see her."

The boy handed her the reins. While he was gone she walked Victorio around the playground, keeping well away from the bushes at the edge that might spook him. She talked to him and patted him, wondering what it would be like to spring up onto his broad back and ride away. Maybe some day!

Too soon, Mom came outside with the boy. She admired Victorio from the porch. Page was reluctant to give up the reins. "I know your horse's name," she said, stalling. "But I don't know yours."

"Doug Allman," he said. "I came to tell your mom about the party Saturday night. It's for her."

At that moment, Saturday night seemed such a long way off Page hardly heard him. "How come you have a horse?" she asked. "I didn't think anybody could have a pet here."

"He stays in the mountain corral with the other horses, but he's my favorite. Dad had to use him this morning. Pretty soon he's going back to the corral, but I thought you'd like to see him."

"Oh, I did, I do!" She looked into Victorio's large trusting eyes. "I wish I could keep him."

"We gotta go now. Want to walk a ways with us?"

Now that Page really looked at the boy, she realized his dad was the board president. He had the same brown eyes and the dimple in his chin.

"That was neat, how you tamed Victorio," he said, as they walked along, Page leading the horse. "He was ready to bolt."

"It was something I've wanted to try for a long time. I'm glad it worked. Please bring him back again."

"I'll show you the corral sometime, if you want."

"Oh, yes! Anytime!" Past Allis's, they came to the Allman's driveway. Now she had to give over the reins. She watched Doug and the horse disappear through the gate in the stone wall surrounding his house. Slowly she walked back to the school, breathing in the horse-and-leather smell of her fingers. Victorio! She couldn't wait to see him again. Carlotta, Domingo, Victorio! She smiled. They sounded like a poem.

Mom was leaning against a porch post watching

the mountains. "It was nice of Doug to bring the horse to see you," she said.

"Oh, sure," Page replied, her smile growing even broader. She didn't care a bit that Doug had really used Victorio as an excuse to meet the new teacher.

9

PAGE WISHED that Saturday night would never come. The welcoming party was set to begin in the mountains at sundown, and she dreaded it. Allis's parents offered to come to the school for them, but Page was late getting ready. She'd had what Mom called an attack of the obstinates, lying on the sofa with her head under a pillow, shouting fierce declarations, ending with, "I refuse to be put on exhibition for a lot of stupid people to stare at! I'd rather stay here by myself!" She knew the pillow muffled most of what she said so Mom wouldn't take offense, and the angry words released some of her pent-up anxiety.

Mom finally tugged the pillow off Page's head and told her in a stern voice to get up and shower. "You don't have to dress fancy, but you're going. Meeting the other kids tonight will make Monday easier for you."

The Lawrence car was waiting at the school's back door when Page stumbled out in the only thing she had to wear to a party, a dark skirt and blouse from the welfare supply room. After greeting Mr. and Mrs. Lawrence, in the front seat with Mom, Page clambered into the back to take her place between Allis and her nine-year-old brother, Clay. As the car headed for the Chisos, she realized why her seat was in the middle. Allis, on her left, nudged her to look at the strange white splotches like spilled paint on top of Lone Mountain. At the same time Clay, on her right, pulled at her sleeve so she'd not miss a coyote skulking in the greasewood. Left to right and back again, Page looked out Allis's window to see Panther Peak from behind, then out Clay's side at an antelope herd racing across the flat.

Allis clapped her hands and announced, "Now! Look ahead—Alsate!"

"No fair!" Clay screeched, waving his hands in front of Page's face to keep her from seeing. "Alsate's on MY side. I get to show her Alsate."

Mr. Lawrence spoke a quiet word over his shoulder, causing Clay to flop back in place. Everybody looked towards Alsate. Page stared with all her might, willing the ghostly Alsate into being. She saw no warrior chief, only more and more desolate mountains with a lavender mist surrounding them, a mist that didn't dim their hard-rock angles.

"I see him!" said Mom. "He's lying down."

"Where? Where?" Page demanded.

"There!" Allis and Clay spoke together, pointing. In the same breath, Allis urged, "Over here! Lost Mine Peak—the silver mine!"

Page stretched her neck to look up, up on Allis's side.

"Green Gulch! Green Gulch!" Clay jiggled her arm. "Panthers all the time!"

"Not ALL the time," Allis corrected him. "But lots of times."

Page looked hard into the gulch. No panthers. She looked hard at Lost Mine Peak. No silver mine. And no Alsate! Maybe she needed glasses. She could see nothing but the same rocks, mountains and stunted greenery that she'd already seen at Panther Flat.

The road now ascended at a steeper angle, and they passed water barrels. "Here's where you get water when your engine overheats," Allis explained.

Page could understand a car rebelling against this curving climb into the Chisos. She felt odd herself, as if she were going deaf. Her ears seemed packed with cotton. Then as the car began descending, her ears gave a painful POP! and she could hear again.

". . . the community center," Clay was saying, pointing down below the road to a frame building in the bowl-shaped valley cuffed by the jagged Chisos. Page caught her breath. What a beautiful scene! But it was a beauty that made her shudder. The red ball of the setting sun hung between a rough V-cut in the mountains to the west. Its clear light, casting no shadows, showed the people getting out of their cars or pickups or jeeps, lifting out their bags and food hampers, and heading toward the weather-worn community center. They took their time getting there, greeting each other, chatting in small groups, with the children darting among them like fleet deer. They looked like brilliantly painted animated dolls. The blue of their clothes was bluer, the red more flaming, the white purer. She hadn't expected so many people. Surely everybody in the park had come, and families from the ranches outside, too.

"Margaret's here," Allis exclaimed with pleasure.

"I see her grandmother's pickup. You'll like Margaret. Belita too, from Dripping Springs."

"And Epifanio. Belita's brother," Clay said, sitting forward to see better. "Here's their dad's truck!"

Mr. Lawrence guided their car in beside it. During the quiet after he switched off the engine, Page panicked—all those strangers, laughing, calling to one another, and joining the party where she would have to meet them.

Allis touched her hand, and said matter-of-factly, "We've moved nine times. I know how it is to be the new person. You always live through it."

Mrs. Lawrence distributed covered dishes for her family to carry. Page and Mom followed them inside. Casseroles, huge salad bowls, and platters stacked with meat—"Roast beef and venison," Allis told her— were arranged on a long table with a steaming caldron of chili as the centerpiece. In the crowd of faces turned toward them Page recognized, with surprise, Jack Spencer. He winked at her. She had been prepared for strangers, yet right away here was someone who seemed like an old friend. Maybe he had brought Domingo. This party might not be so bad after all.

Someone else who caught Page's attention looked like a female pirate, her towering figure draped in purple and red, big gold loops dangling from ears that were set tight against her head. Her coal black hair, piled in tiers, was held in place by a gold-knobbed hair pin. Lipstick made a scarlet slash in her sun-wrinkled face. Gold rings sparked with large green stones weighed down her blunt-fingered hands, and gold shoes glimmered under her long skirt. Page hadn't expected to see anyone like this, and yet, why not? From what little she'd learned about the Big Bend's history, this woman fit right in.

"Who's that?" she whispered to Clay, beside her.

He followed her gaze, and said, without lowering his voice, "Gypsy Meg. And there's Epifanio!" He rushed off to join his friend.

Later when Mr. Spencer came over, she asked about Domingo.

"I didn't bring him. He'd have to stay shut up in the car alone. That's no fun." He squinted his eyes, examining her face. "How's everything going?" He sounded as if he really wanted to know. That made Page speak more truthfully than she might have otherwise.

"Not too awful," she admitted. "The board decided I can stay if I don't interfere with Mom's work."

"And have you interfered?"

"A little," she confessed, thinking of her tantrums.

"Take good care of her," he said. "Her job isn't easy."

Just then Billy Newhouse, looking as rumpled as when she'd first seen him, sidled through the crowd and thrust a paper bag at her. "From Carlotta," he whispered.

Page reached in and took hold of a black rope that seemed to have no end. She stretched her arm full length overhead, and there was still more of it coming out of the bag. Anise fumes were so strong Page could almost see them. "Licorice! How did Carlotta know I'm crazy about licorice?" The men laughed and moved away to make room for the kids crowding around Page.

She handed around the licorice rope for each one to pull off a piece. With blackened teeth and sticky fingers they stood in a loose group talking and laughing as if they were old friends. The candy made a dreaded ordeal as easy for Page as counting to five. Had Billy Newhouse known it would? Page's grateful eyes sought him at the other end of the long room talking to Mom and Jack Spencer. As Page watched, who should join them but Jame, looking lean and courtly in his denims. She half expected the cook and the waiter to barge through the door, but she knew they'd probably be watching or playing football on a Saturday night.

With a grin, she turned back to the kids and the comforting scent of anise. Now they were pulling the remainder of the rope into a slim string, passing the end of it from sticky hand to sticky hand, twisting and kneading until it stretched around their circle from Page to Allis, then to Belita, Kathy, Doug, Clay, Kathy's sister Mary, Margaret from down-river, and Belita's brother, Epifanio.

While they tied a licorice bow for decorating the wall, Page inventoried the missing pupils: the cowboy and the ranch kid, but they weren't expected because of the distance and the roads bad for night driving; the Hill boy, whose parents didn't want the board to hire Mom; and Hank Boatwright, the former teacher's son. She understood why they didn't come, but what about Bart and Bret? They were such live wires, she'd thought they wouldn't miss a party for any reason. Like cheerleaders, they acted enthusiastic about everything. They hadn't mentioned that their parents were against Mom. What did their absence mean?

Her puzzling was cut short by lines forming on both sides of the table loaded with food. After serving themselves, the kids took their plates outside to picnic tables. Between bites, the younger ones ran around playing, while the older ones told Page about the Big Bend.

They act as if they own the place, she thought impatiently. That's the way the twins talked on the Indian camp hike, and Allis and Clay on the way over here. I could never care that much about a pile of rocks and some dried-out cactus plants. Her arms still stung from tangling with the catclaw bush.

"See the horse stalls up there?" Doug pointed to what, in the twilight, looked like a row of rock stalls on the side of a mountain.

"Are they real? Something the Spanish soldiers left?" Page asked.

Allis laughed with the others. "No, they're natural," she said.

"She likes horses," Doug said, and told them about Page's mysterious communication with Victorio. The others paused in their eating to look at her, impressed.

"I have a book that tells how to talk to animals," she told them, embarrassed but pleased. "Where's the corral?"

"Up the mountain a ways," Epifanio said.

"Let's take her there," someone suggested.

"Lots of horses," Kathy said. "Sometimes they work on the trails."

"Tourists rent them, too," Belita added.

"And Victorio is the top horse!" At Doug's proclamation, he and Page exchanged smiles.

"Let's go!" Page said, impatient to see the chestnut horse again.

"If there's time," Allis agreed. The bigger kids speeded up their eating.

Dainty, blond Margaret, scraping her plate, said, "May I borrow that book? I want to talk to animals."

Page's heart gave a squeeze. In the excitement she had forgotten the book was back home—if Dad still had their home. She held her voice steady though, and answered, "I left it in Alabama. When I get it, I'll lend it to you."

"You wish to talk to Carmencita?" Belita asked Margaret in precise English.

Margaret nodded, explaining to Page, "That's my grandma's mountain lion." Before Page could recover from her astonishment, Mrs. Lawrence called them to come for dessert. In the scramble to help the smaller children tidy up, and the rush inside, Page made a mental note about the horse corral and Margaret's grandmother. She searched the crowd around the dessert table for someone small-boned and fair like Margaret. Nobody fit that description.

"As soon as Clete comes, square dancing will start," Doug said, his cheek crammed with cookies.

"That's what's fun," Allis smiled out over the crowd. "Everybody joins in."

"The little ones too?" Page couldn't believe it.

"Yeah," said Epifanio, his white smile wide in his coffee-colored face. "Whoever wants to, dances." He tapped the toe of his boot in a rapid tattoo.

Belita nodded agreement, her dark eyes shining.

Everybody turned toward the door when Clete entered. Page knew who he was though no one called a name. Long and lithe, he seemed to glide into the room the way she imagined a panther would, a rare black panther. His skin, burned dark as mahogany by the sun, contrasted vividly with his snow white shirt. Keen black eyes flashed above high wide cheekbones centered with a hook nose, making him look like a Comanche chief stepping from the pages of the Big Bend legend book. A cruel face, Page thought, remembering how the peaceful river Indians dreaded the Mexico Moon.

"Where's your fiddle?" Doug shouted, rushing toward him. The other boys followed, clamoring around him like a pack of pet hounds. Somebody took his white roll-brimmed hat. Somebody else brought him a heaped plate. Page couldn't hear anything he said because of the noise, and she lost sight of him when he sat down.

But she saw Margaret, taking another brownie from the dessert table, and remembered what she meant to do. "Where's your grandma? Can I meet her?"

"Sure. Let's take her one of these," and she chose another brownie, wrapping it in a paper napkin. Then to Page's astonishment Margaret led her to the least likely person to be grandmother to this delicate, blond girl—Gypsy Meg!

10

GYPSY MEG'S BOOMING LAUGH shook her large frame as she watched the expression on Page's face.

"Believe it or not, I'm this little glutton's granny. Welcome to the Big Bend, Page." She extended her hand, jingling a dozen gold bracelets. Her handshake was brisk.

Page could think of nothing to say except what loomed most important in her mind, "Do you really have a mountain lion?"

"Most certainly I do. What would you like to know about her?"

"Everything! Where did you get it? Is it dangerous? What does it eat? Where—"

"Un momentito!" Gypsy Meg interrupted. "I think we don't have time to go into all that now. The dancing is ready." She glanced at Margaret, who had finished the crumbs of her brownie, and was now pinching bits off her grandmother's. "Come visit us. You will see Carmencita for yourself. Would that please you?"

"I'd like that, if Margaret would."

"She will. So will I, and Carmencita."

A few strokes of Clete's fiddle bow alerted everyone. The music began, peppy and prancy. Gypsy Meg's skirts swung in rhythm to it and her snapping eyes looked beyond Page to where the square dance was

forming. Margaret took the last bite of her grand-mother's dessert and wiped her fingers on the napkin.

"How was my chocolate treat you so generously brought me?" Gypsy Meg asked.

"Delicious!" Margaret said, without embarrass-ment. "I'll get you another one."

"No, you won't," Gypsy Meg said, restraining her. "You'll only eat it also. Enough! Now we dance." She beckoned the girls to follow her as she swayed across the floor to join the others, her gold feet impatient beneath the purple and red skirt.

Page stayed behind. The whirling action that shook the building, the shouts of the caller whose strong voice could be heard clearly over the pounding feet and the laughter, dazzled her. The spirited fiddling cast a buoyant spell on her clumsy feet, which kept time to the music without her permission.

She watched Mom in amazement. How did she know what to do? Maybe because the older people and the more expert ones looked out for the others. Once she noticed Mom standing alone and bewil-dered, then out of the melee appeared Jame who swung her around and on to the next partner. All ages and sizes managed to heed the caller with few mis-steps. When a mix-up occurred, everyone laughed and regrouped to continue.

What a lot of calories they're burning, Page thought. No wonder Margaret's brownies don't show on her.

When intermission came, Jack Spencer urged her to join the dancing. Page said no, knowing that she'd make too many mistakes and ruin the dance for everybody. Besides, she felt overloaded with things to think about. She had to get away. Slipping outside, she found a place to sit against the wall in the chill dark. She couldn't believe that not far from her at this moment was a corral full of horses, and that the kids had promised to take her there! She would see Victorio again. Gypsy Meg had invited her to visit a mountain lion! Could this be dumb, clumsy Page Williams sitting here in the heart of the Chisos Mountains, with so many adventures waiting to happen to her? Was this the same girl she had been for twelve years, but who was now surrounded by treasure caves, and haunted by spirits—Spanish soldiers, Comanches, Mescalero Apaches, and basket weavers? At this moment, they seemed as real to Page as the merry-making in the room back of her.

Day after tomorrow, would school actually begin in this strange place? She shivered, wanting to hold fast to this Saturday night, at the same time yearning to rush ahead to see what next week, next month would bring. Fearful, yet excited, she stared into the dark as if she could glimpse the future out there.

Two shadows moving past recalled her to the present. They went to the lighted window and, standing well back, spied inside. Keeping still, she flared her nostrils the way Victorio did, scenting them. They smelled like a mixture of dust, creosote bushes, and stale sweat. Why did their sweat make her want to cough, when horse sweat made her breathe deeper?

She studied them—teenage boys, typical of the Big Bend, their wide-brimmed hats pulled low to shadow their faces. The taller boy carried something in his off-hand which Page couldn't see clearly, something black that was long and slender. Not a rifle, more like a fishing pole, but not that either. After a short while of intent watching, he whispered, "Now. Let's do it now." Without another sound they faded into the night.

Page remained where she sat, too scared to move, knowing the boys could still be watching from the darkness. Their stealthy manner, hats tilted low on their foreheads, along with the taller boy's ominous whisper, made her want to stay hidden. The second boy's unquestioned acceptance of the decision, and the businesslike way they went about carrying it out, showed they had planned well.

A shattering sound brought Page to her feet—a mountain splitting open or a lightning strike. Silence. Then she heard a terrible cry. It sounded like the Big Bend book's description of Comanche and Apache warriors thundering into a no-quarters battle against each other. No survivors, no mercy. Reading the description in the old book had chilled Page. Hearing the cry was paralyzing.

After a frozen moment, Page fumbled her way back into the lighted hall. No one there had heard anything. The music, dancing, and laughing continued as before.

Mr. Allman, refilling his glass at the refreshment table, saw Page. Immediately, he came to her.

"What is it?" The concern in his voice caused Page to focus her eyes on him.

"Something," she gasped, "something terrible."

Gradually quiet fell and movement stilled as the others took notice of them. Clete held the fiddle bow in midair, the instrument under his chin. Everyone, looking toward Page and Mr. Allman, heard the pounding feet, and saw the wild-eyed cowboy who burst through the door.

"The horses!" he shouted. "The corral is busted, and the horses spooked!"

The men left their partners standing on the dance floor and headed toward the door. Then the lights went out. The blackest black Page had ever seen gripped the party. For all that she could see and hear, she stood alone in an immensity of black. Then a sound like an indrawn breath swept over the room. A young child wailed, triggering loud exclamations and questions no one could answer.

"Quiet, everyone! Quiet!" thundered Mr. Allman. "Now, listen!" He instructed those who had flashlights or lanterns in their vehicles to get them. "Move with care," he warned them. He named men to check the generator, others to check the switch box, and the rest to remain in place for the time being. Some of the women rummaged in the kitchen drawers and found candles. In the flickering light, Page looked around at the tense faces, not yet recovered from the fright of sudden darkness. The children found places to sit, and kept quiet while emergency measures were taken.

Through the window Page watched the car lights springing on. Soon family groups, minus the fathers, gathered their food containers and lighted the way to their cars with the flashlights. The men bunched near the door, ready to start a roundup of the stampeded horses.

Page realized several things as Mrs. Lawrence drove carefully down the mountains and back to Panther Flat. She, Page, was a near witness to the destructive deed and certainly a witness to the deed-doers. In Green Gulch, the many eyes reflecting their car lights reminded her that panthers, lovers of horseflesh, roved the Big Bend night, where Victorio and the other terrified horses would be easy prey. Unlike the earlier ride over, those in the car had little to say, absorbed as they were in their own wondering.

At the school, she and Mom were relieved to find everything in order. They quickly got ready for bed and turned off the light. Page could not sleep, however. After an endless time of lying rigid beside Mom, she slithered onto the floor, and crept to the window.

She sat watching the hubcap, and thinking of what she knew that no one else knew, or suspected, about two boys she'd never seen in the light. Would she know them if she met them? She cringed to think of what it would mean if she told—how much trouble she would cause, how displeased the school board would be with her causing trouble, how everyone would look at her and question her. She felt weighed down with anxiety. How could Victorio and the other horses be rescued in this dark wilderness? The men could be hurt or even killed trying to find them, men who had been kind to her and Mom, men who were dads to kids she was now friends with.

Shadows came and went at the water pan. Page scarcely noticed the six small skunks walking primly in a straight line, led by one handsome parent and followed by the other. They gathered around the water and took their time drinking. A bony kit fox, its pointed face and large ears silhouetted in the dark, waited a respectful distance until the skunks finished and left in their neat single file. Page felt too distracted to get excited over them tonight. Finally, with numb feet, she slipped back into bed and fell asleep.

11

PAGE AWAKENED LATE on Sunday morning. Mom still slept even though the apartment was bright with sunshine. Everything that happened last night reclaimed her thoughts immediately. She was not tempted to lie in bed today. She had to be up and dressed, watching the houses across the arroyo for clues to last night's outcome.

She took bread and jam to the patio and ate while keeping surveillance over the immense countryside. She saw nothing until a panelled truck towing a refrigerator trailer turned in on the Panther Flat road. This must be the grocery delivery rig. She remembered hearing last night that Cleofas would be bringing it today because Billy Newhouse came yesterday for the party.

When the strange vehicle took the schoolhouse road, she hurried inside where Mom was groping about the kitchen, eyes half open, making breakfast. They went to meet Cleofas on the playground to help bring in the groceries. He couldn't tell them any news because theirs was the first stop he had made.

After he left, Page and Mom stood admiring all the groceries covering the counter, the stove top, and piled on the floor. For the first time the little refrigerator would be filled, and the cupboard shelves loaded.

"How rich we are," Page rejoiced.

"Yes," Mom agreed, smiling. "Now I feel secure."

They took their time organizing the food supply, anticipating the meals they would cook. When they finished, they set to work making the school ready for tomorrow. Having many things to do usually made the time fly, but to Page it was one of the longest days she'd lived. She saw no one, not even at a distance, so her suspense about last night went unrelieved. Too weary to enjoy the supper Mom made from the new grocery supply, Page fell into bed and was asleep before she could worry about Victorio or opening day tomorrow.

Next morning she made sure she was finished with breakfast and out on the playground when the kids began arriving. First the Panther Flat students came walking in, carrying their lunch boxes, all except Hank Boatwright who was sick with flu, one of the twins reported.

"Mack Hill's sick too," Doug added.

Then those from up in the mountains, who had picked up the Dripping Springs people along the way, were followed by Margaret, delivered by her grandmother in the pickup.

Everybody talked about Saturday night, and nothing else. Page listened, trying to piece the fragments into a whole. What they knew added up to an unknown someone opening the corral gate, and by unknown means panicking the horses. That same person, or perhaps another unknown person working with him, had cut the power line to the community center. All the horses except three had been rounded up and were back in the corral. Two were still missing, and a third had been hurt so severely it had to be shot.

Fear made Page's hands clammy. She was wild to ask about Victorio, but she shrank from calling attention to herself. Someone might suddenly remember that she had given the first alarm, only seconds before the wrangler burst into the community center. From what the kids said, he had been yarning with some tourists around the lodge fireplace when, through the window, he glimpsed horses flashing past the lighted concessions area. That was the first moment he knew that something was wrong. Was it possible no one else saw the two boys prowling in the dark? Or that no one else heard those piercing sounds echoing against the mountains?

While they stood together rehashing the events of Saturday night, she watched Doug's face, thinking that surely he would show some distress if Victorio had been hurt or killed. His face was calm, but he listened intently.

The ranch pickup rolled in at a dignified speed, and parked carefully at the back side of the playground. All talk stopped and everyone turned to watch it. The passenger door opened, and a boy in western garb slid to the ground.

"Sam," said Bret/Bart.

"Third grade," added his brother.

Out of the driver's side stretched boots and long jean-clad legs, followed by a denim shirt, and then the usual sombrero ducked to clear the door. When the cowboy figure straightened up, Page's eyes widened at his height. He looked full grown, yet he was in first grade! Without hesitating, he glanced toward their group and smiled, teeth white and strong in his sun-browned face.

"Travis," the boys breathed, their eyes big with awe.

Now somebody else came out of the passenger side, somebody unexpected who turned on her stomach, reaching her short legs toward the ground, a small girl with curly blond hair.

"Lily," explained Sam, approaching the gawking group. "She's staying with us during the week so she can come to school."

The electric bell buzzed, an alien sound in the Panther Flat morning. It seemed to set the girls free to surround Lily, offering to take her hand, to carry her lunch box, and her book satchel. Lily smiled at them, her big eyes lavender as the Chisos at dawn, her creamy cheeks dimpling. But she shook off all helping hands.

"I'll do it myself," she said, holding her possessions close.

Page trailed in last, wondering how Travis would affect the school. She knew Mom was worried about him, that he might be defiant toward her, and influence the other kids to resist her teaching. If Page's first impression proved true, Travis posed no problem.

No problem, that is, except he was far too big for his desk, and Lily was much too small for it, so neither student in first grade had a place to sit. Mom cleared one end of the library table for Travis. Allis went across the arroyo and returned with a footstool for Lily to sit on. At least it allowed her feet to touch the floor.

Later, Mrs. Lawrence appeared at the door carrying a short-legged table with a drawer, which delighted Lily. Mom set it near Travis, and there they were—the strangest looking first grade in existence—Lily, tiny and flouncy with a lace-edged handkerchief folded in her pocket, tall Travis with his saddle-worn jeans and rough-knuckled hands, both dead serious about learning. They would be even more unusual when Jesús, the boy from Mexico, started coming. Belita said he would begin school as soon as the river lowered enough for him to ride a burro across to the U.S. She added, "He is my cousin. He will stay at my house at Dripping Springs in the week-time. On the Saturdays and the Sundays he will return home to Mexico."

12

PAGE HAD MUCH TO THINK ABOUT as the first days of school passed, days of adjustment to new names and faces, of carrying out her assignments without being distracted by the other grades studying theirs, of learning the routine of a one-room school. Back of all the situations that Page had to respond to hovered the mystery of last Saturday night. Her efforts to make sense of what she had seen and heard produced no answers. Not knowing Victorio's fate was the hardest part, but she believed the risk of drawing attention to herself by asking about him was too great.

By Friday afternoon she was almost convinced that nobody remembered her involvement in the party tragedy. She felt so sure that she barely glanced up from her notes when Doug's dad appeared at the school door. But suddenly she realized Mom and Mr. Allman were looking at her as if her name had been called. Mom said, "Will you step outside? Mr. Allman wants to talk with you."

Her insides scrunched into a knot the way her toes did on skunk night. How hard it was to leave her desk and follow him to the porch. His face and voice were kind as he questioned her. He mentioned her abrupt return to the party, and how he had come over to her. "What frightened you? Why did you say what you said?"

Clinging to a post, Page looked off toward the Chisos, remembering that night. But something else she remembered was the school board's request of Mom not to cause trouble, to keep the peace. And Mom had promised the board that Page would make no trouble. More than that, after that board meeting, Page herself had promised that she would make no trouble.

"You must have seen something," Mr. Allman insisted. "This was a dangerous thing that happened—dangerous to the horses, which are valuable to us, and dangerous to the men who had to round them up in the dark."

He waited.

Page ran her tongue over dry lips. "I was outside. Just sitting, in the dark."

Mr. Allman stood quietly, not pressing her. That made it easier for her thoughts to leapfrog what she'd seen, and go on to what she'd heard.

"In just a little while, a noise—my head felt split open. Then some kind of shriek . . ."

"What kind of noise? What did it remind you of?"

"Sharp. Cracking. Loud." She shook her head at her inability to be more exact.

"The shriek. What was that like?"

"Like a Comanche war cry, going in for the attack. . . ." She shivered remembering how the legend book had described the savage cry that proclaimed no mercy to humans or animals.

"A human cry?"

She looked at him, surprised. "Yes. Human, but wild."

He half turned away, and they both stared at the Chisos range, which seemed to hold its secrets closer in the clear afternoon light.

"If you remember anything else that might help, please tell me. So far we have little to go on."

Here was Page's chance to ask about Victorio, but now she knew that she feared the answer. She'd rather not know till she had to know.

Mr. Allman gave her a quick smile and said, "Thanks."

She returned to class unhappy because of the key information she'd kept from him, but certain her decision had been right. She looked at Mom now, working at the blackboard with the seventh graders. Page had never seen her so full of sparkle, despite the hard work of teaching so many grades and running the school. She vowed again to do what she could to give Mom her chance, to help her succeed as a teacher here.

Later, Page likened the first month of school to a steeplechase hurdle. What made it so hard to get over the obstacle course was her knowledge of some things she wished she didn't know, and her ignorance of other things that she needed to know: routine in a one-room school where so much went on at the same time, how to get her homework done as well as her janitor duties, and how to make a place for herself among her spirited western classmates. Though they were few, the kids came from very different backgrounds. Most of them had grown up in national parks, and their families had lived in all parts of the country. Those who had never left the Big Bend were just as interesting—most of them lean and tan from outdoor living. They seemed self-assured with each other and adults alike. Page noticed they could always think up things to do and games to play.

Margaret and Lily were different from the others. On some days Margaret didn't play; she sat in the shade looking more tired than usual. Lily was always in the center of whatever activity was going on, wearing ruffled dresses, a lacy handkerchief tucked in the pocket, and ribbons in her blond curls.

Mixed teams of boys and girls played kickball during free time. They had made up their own rules, and it seemed to Page the rules were flexible. She laughed to herself watching a game in progress, the kids kicking the ball with their cowboy boots, toes upturned, and then running with their sombreros sitting securely in place, brims gently rolled upward, blue-jeaned legs churning across the dusty playground. Page thought of the wide-brimmed hat, faded jeans, and scuffed boots as the Big Bend uniform.

Most of the time everyone got along well. The quarrels erupted when the girls tired of kickball and wanted to swing or play with each other. That left the boys without enough players for two teams, and they argued with the girls to come back.

Once they had their science courses underway, the weeks passed for Page more like a thoroughbred running on the straightaway. Every grade worked on the solar system, but at different levels. Mom ordered more science books, this time from the state library system. Mr. Spencer delivered them at recess time. While he and Mom had coffee in the kitchen, the kids played with Domingo in the cleared space in the middle of the schoolroom. The little dog was willing to play with the others, but always his place of safety was with Page.

By this time Hank Boatwright and Mack Hill had recovered from the "flu." Page was perplexed that everyone knew the boys hadn't been sick, that their parents kept them out to protest the new teacher. Why didn't somebody admit it? Probably this was an unspoken way they united to keep the peace. So far Page had seen no outward signs of animosity toward her and Mom, but she realized that the boys' late start put them behind in their school assignments and Mom had to work harder giving them extra help. More than likely that was another purpose for keeping them out of school—anything to complicate life for the new teacher.

Page realized the minute the two boys walked in that they were the ones who had stood at the community center window that night. Looking at them, she'd never think they would do such a mean and dangerous thing. They both wore open-faced expressions, their manner modest. Hank was taller. He kept his dark hair neatly combed and seemed to be especially careful of his powerful looking hands. Anywhere that he had to wait his turn he spent the time flexing his wrists and stretching his arms so that the muscles bulged. Mack's fair-skinned blond coloring and wide-open blue eyes gave an impression of innocence. Page noticed that when he talked to Mom his pink mouth

curved up in a half smile. The two boys did not re-
semble each other physically, yet to Page they
seemed alike, perhaps because of their matching
eager-to-please expressions.

Neither boy gave any hint that he planned mischief,
but mischief happened. Second grader Kathy's lunch
disappeared, to be found, after a search, in the supply
closet where Kathy had never gone. Doug's lost homework was in the wastepaper basket when Page emptied
it at the close of the school day. Allis's model of Jupiter,
made of papier-mâché for the solar system mobile,
turned up dented and with three moons missing.

No one saw these things happening, but Allis,
flushed with indignation, glared at Mack and Hank,
her suspicions plain on her face. Page suggested that
the Chisos ghosts were active, which broke the ten-
sion a little and caused some laughter.

Two who were never bothered by the boys were
Page and Travis. They treated Page as if she didn't ex-
ist, and they kept their distance from Travis. She felt
a certain security because the boys didn't know she
knew what they'd done. She was often troubled because she hadn't told anyone, but how could she?
What proof did she have? No doubt at all that Mack
Hill and Hank Boatwright were the ones who stampeded the horses. But how did they make those eerie
sounds like the earth splitting open? That cry like a
savage war whoop?

She had no chance to talk to Doug outside of
school, and during school she couldn't ask him about
Victorio without everyone hearing. But one day when
lunch hour was almost over she saw him standing at

the edge of the arroyo looking across at headquarters. As she came up to him she was struck by the tenseness of his body and the pinched look around his mouth that made him look old.

She barged into his thoughts with her question because she couldn't wait any longer. "Do you know anything about Victorio?"

Doug's eyes didn't waver from whatever he was watching in the distance. "No. My dad doesn't hear me when I ask. And my mom says don't bother him."

"You think he doesn't want to tell you?" Page asked with a tremor in her voice.

"I mean to find out. That's the wrangler's jeep over there now. When he leaves, I'm going to catch him. I gotta know."

Page remembered how high-strung Victorio was, how easily spooked. What he had heard suddenly in the dark that night could terrify him enough to stampede him over a cliff. No, no—not Victorio! She lingered long enough to see Doug hurrying down into the arroyo to intercept the jeep. The bell rang and she went inside, her chest tight with apprehension.

Time passed and Doug didn't come back. Mom went outside, but returned alone. She asked uneasily if anyone knew what happened to Doug. Had he gone home? Nobody offered any information. From the window Page looked across the arroyo at the road where the wrangler's jeep would have passed. Doug wasn't in sight. Mom went outside again. Page heard her calling. When she returned this time, she stood by her desk biting her lip and frowning in thought.

"Teacher," Lily said, "I lost my handkerchief at dinnertime. May I go look for it?"

Mom readied her mouth to say no, but then she nodded. "Take Jesús with you," she added.

Sometime later the two first graders came back grinning, Lily waving her handkerchief. She worked at her desk awhile, then suddenly announced, "Doug is in the arroyo eating burny beans."

Mom whirled on her. "Burny beans? What do you mean?"

"They're poison," Travis said, his eyes wide.

"Deadly," Allis said. "You're not supposed to even touch a burny bean."

"He's crying," Lily added.

"Travis, will you go see?" Mom asked. "Hurry!"

Page leaped to her feet. "Let me," she pleaded, looking from Mom to Travis. The tears in her eyes must have convinced them she should be the one to go. She sped down in the arroyo along the path she had seen Doug take.

Page heard him before she saw him, savagely kicking a boulder and pounding it with his fists. Tears poured down his twisted face, and he sobbed out fierce words that terrified her. She understood how he felt but she could focus her rage and grief on the two boys responsible while Doug had no one to blame. As out of control as he was, maybe it was better that he hadn't.

She saw he was hurting himself, though he didn't seem to feel the pain, or to know that she was there. She searched about for a stick. They were few and far between, but she found a stout dried-out stem of cholla, which she grabbed and forced into his sweating and bloody fist. "Beat! Beat! I'll help you," she shouted in his ear, snatching a stick for herself. They flailed and beat and cried. When the sticks hung in limp shreds, they sank against the boulder, exhausted.

"My mom said come," she snuffled into her shirt-tail, wiping her face. "She's worried."

Without answering, he followed her up the steep side of the arroyo. "Wash your face," she ordered, making her voice threatening. "If you don't come out by the time I wash mine, I'll come in for you." When she'd finished in the girls' bathroom, he was drinking from the fountain. Together they went inside. Mom took one look at Doug and came toward him, concern sharpening her face. Page shook her head in a warning to back off, and Mom reluctantly resumed the lesson she was teaching.

Doug spent the rest of the day staring out the window. Page accomplished little herself. Her eyes often strayed to the two boys who were unaware that she knew they were responsible for killing Victorio. The hatred that welled up inside her must have sent shock waves across the schoolroom because both boys, who had never looked at her before, were clearly startled to catch her supercharged gaze on them. Immediately she looked down, realizing two things: she must not let them suspect she knew, and she must not cause trouble for Mom.

13

NO MATTER WHAT WORRIES Page struggled with, she always smiled to see the first grade studying their ABCs together. Travis squatted beside Lily's table, both of them tense with concentration, helping each other learn the letters. Sometimes they worked at the blackboard, at other times, especially when cutting out or pasting, they spread their equipment on the floor. Travis put his whole heart into whatever the first grade had to do, and made it such fun the other students wished they could be first graders too.

Jesús, not much larger than Lily, joined in their activities with enthusiasm when he finally started coming to school. He spoke no English, but Travis, who was fluent in Spanish, interpreted for him and Mom. On the playground he communicated well enough without English, and was as rough and tumble as the rest of them.

Studying the solar system appealed to everyone, Page thought, because the sky dominated the Big Bend world, holding the mountains, the flats, the arroyos, and the river in their proper places. So far-flung it had no limits in daylight, at night it seemed within reaching distance if you just stood on tiptoe. In the

mornings the sun seemed to hurl itself up from behind the Dead Horse, and at night to plummet back of
the Chisos in a blaze of clouds that lighted the world
for a long time afterwards.

What they learned about how the solar system
worked took the mystery out of what they observed
but didn't lessen its fascination for them. Rainbows,
double and single, they could watch from the school
window. They learned the colors: red, orange, yellow,
green, blue, indigo, violet. "ROY G BIV"—Lily and
Jesús liked to chant the acronym Mom taught them
for remembering the order of the colors. Everybody
sooner or later painted a rainbow, or created one out
of bits of colored paper. The wall facing the windows
was lined with rainbow artwork.

One afternoon Travis returned from the porch
drinking fountain to report a different kind of rainbow hovering over the Chisos. With every rainbow
they had ever seen, they had stood between the bow
and the sun—when they looked at one, they had their
backs to the other. But this ordinary cloud, suspended
between them and the western sun, was transformed
into a blob-shaped rainbow that gave Page a creepy
feeling.

"Notice it's over Panther Peak," Allis whispered.
That was where the legend book claimed a cache of
gold bars lay hidden, in a horseshoe-shaped canyon
marked by a hundred-foot waterfall. Was this rainbow
more than a freak of nature? Was it a signal for them?
Page believed it.

Mom led them to talk about how the water
droplets in the cloud acted as prisms to separate the

sun's rays into the various ROY G BIV colors the same way as in the usual arching rainbow. The pupils clustered on the playground, watching the cloud and discussing it, when Mack Hill's mother drove in and parked. Page knew her immediately—her blond and pink coloring matched his. She wore the prettiest dress Page had seen in Texas, and her shoes, high-heeled with straps, the least sensible. Page admired the delicate gold chain around her ankle, and the way she arched her feet as she walked toward their group. Page liked looking at Mrs. Hill until she spoke.

"Is school out early today?" Her voice twanged through her nose.

"We're studying science," Mack told her with a little grimace.

"See the rainbow cloud?" Allis pointed.

Mrs. Hill didn't look. "I suppose since you're out here, Mack wouldn't miss anything if I took him home now."

Mom invited her in to see their science projects. Page tried looking at the room through a visitor's eyes—pretty would be her impression, with lots of color and interesting things to see. The prism broke up the white light into dancing colors. The papier-mâché mobile of the solar system swung from the ceiling on invisible nylon threads. Paintings and collages covered the wall opposite the windows, and diagrams and charts filled the bulletin board. The calendar they were making showed the phases of the moon and the seasons of the year, and a model brought the lunar landscape to life.

She watched Mrs. Hill to see if her reaction was

similar. Clearly, it was not. With folded arms she stood just inside the door while Mack collected his homework and lunch box. They left without saying goodbye.

How could she be that way, Page wondered. I should be the one mad about all these projects because I have to clean up the glop and the glue and the paint that spills over. But even so I like to look at everything.

Page often rested her eyes from reading by staring into the infinite depths of the paintings. Each was very different from the others, yet showed the same solar system. Other times she turned in the opposite direction and lost herself staring toward the Dead Horse range and beyond. Travis called it the *Sierra del Caballo Muerto* in the musical Spanish that Page liked to hear.

Another day Mrs. Boatwright found them on the playground, laughing as they chose students to represent the planets, and arranging themselves in orbit around Travis, the sun. Lily was Pluto at the far edge of the enormous playground which symbolized the solar system. Beyond Lily, the thousands of acres of the park represented outer space. Page, Earth, and Allis, Earth's moon, shook with giggling fits as they did their rotating and revolving at the same time. Mom, like the director of a grand pageant, got them going, each planet or moon moving at its relative speed.

Mrs. Boatwright reacted like Mrs. Hill, frowning in disapproval, as if they were wasting time. "I brought Hank a pack of paper," she said to Mom. "What for I don't know as you don't seem to do much written work."

"He'll need it," said Mom. "We use a great deal of paper, especially now that we're keeping a 'heavenly journal.' Will you stay for while?"

"I've no time. But I hope you are teaching the really important subjects—arithmetic, reading, and spelling. Penmanship, too. When I was the teacher, I drilled them every day."

"Oh, yes, we work on those subjects too," Mom assured her. Mrs. Boatwright didn't wait around to hear any more. Mom looked troubled before turning her attention to the solar system again. Some of the fun was gone now, and they soon went inside after Mom promised they'd work on it another day.

Mom pointed out to the students that the night sky in the Big Bend was perfect for studying the stars especially during the dark of the moon. That's where their "heavenly journal" came in. At home they jotted down their observations of the sky and then compared notes at school.

"Keep an exact record of when the sun rises and when it sets," Mom stressed. "Be sure you keep the dates accurately."

Sometimes parents brought their kids back to the school after supper and, sitting on the patio, they figured out the constellations and watched for meteors. They used the star map off the schoolroom wall to help identify what they saw. They studied the sky through binoculars, hoping to discover a comet. The most famous night, the one Page knew she'd never forget, was the time the great full moon rose from behind the Dead Horse and the earth's shadow moved across its face to create a total eclipse. The excitement and suspense of waiting for the moon stole everybody's attention from the skunks, the kit foxes, the deer, and mountain lions moving about in the darkness that enveloped the school. A glow above the mountain range, growing in intensity, warned them the moon was on its way.

"But remember," Mom cautioned, "the moon is not rising. The earth is turning toward the moon so that we come into a position to see it." Page found that hard to accept after a lifetime of watching the moon "rise." She got a woozy feeling imagining the mountains spinning, spinning through space with all of them sitting on this patio following close behind. When the moon's upper edge showed above the top of the mountain range, everyone let out a long "Ahhhhhh!" almost like a groan. They watched what followed, as if bound in a spell that kept them from moving or speaking.

As the earth's round-edged shadow moved across the great orange moon, Mom said softly, "Can you see why early astronomers could know the shape of our world?" A general murmuring of agreement and of marvel washed over the group. The moon glowed like a red ember veiled by the earth's shadow, and the Big Bend lay still and silent beneath it.

They stayed till the last of the shadow slipped off the edge of the moon leaving it a large metallic disk that obscured every star in the eastern sky with its hard white light. How mysterious and wonderful the Big Bend appeared that night. Page wondered if the devil's witches had danced during the eclipse, or had they too been struck still?

After the group scattered to their homes, Page stood alone on the school porch watching the Chisos. Of all nights for the spirits of the Chisos to wander, this should be the one. She wished she knew what was happening in the canyon that she and Allis had decided must be the right one—the horseshoe-shaped canyon that led into the heart of Panther Peak. According to the legend book, the cave was so near the spectacular waterfall that searchers could not talk to one another because of the roar. Ever since the unusual rainbow appeared, the two girls had believed that out of all the possible locations for the lost cache of gold bars this had to be the right one.

Allis's parents forbade them hiking to this particular canyon. They said such a rough trek required an adult along for safety. Privately, Page and Allis stewed and complained. Publicly, they searched for an adult willing to undertake an arduous, all-day hike. So far they hadn't found anyone willing, but tonight, as Page watched the Chisos starkly highlighted by the full moon, she felt certain that the canyon, the cave, and the treasure were there waiting, marked by the rainbow cloud.

The kids from up in the Chisos brought news to school one morning of a hiker lost in the mountains. Mary and Kathy reported they had been playing outside their house late the afternoon before when they heard somebody shouting from far away.

"It sounded like somebody hollering 'help,' but we weren't sure." The sisters had called their parents to come out and listen. They, too, thought the voice sounded desperate. Their father went for a ranger without delay, because dark was coming on fast, and nights were cold now.

"The ranger said nobody had been reported missing," Belita added to the story because she and Epifanio had been waiting at the tourist lodge for their dad to come from work. "But he did find out about a camper who had not been seen for two days. Another camper said when she last saw him, he was on his way to climb Emory Peak."

"Alone?" said Allis. "And without telling the rangers?"

"That's over 7,000 feet," Hank Boatwright said. "Even I've never climbed that one."

"Those are the people who always get in trouble," Mack Hill said self-righteously.

"He sure is in trouble. If that's who it is," Epifanio said. "The search party started out at first light this morning to look for him. Our dad went with them. They think the man must be hurt because his voice comes from the same place every time."

"And his voice is getting weaker," supplied Kathy.

Page wondered what it would be like to be stranded in the Chisos for days and nights, hurt or for some reason unable to hike out. She waited eagerly to hear developments. The man wasn't found the first day of the search, and no cries for help could be heard anymore. Evidence confirmed he was the missing camper. Another frosty night passed, with the searchers going out again the following morning.

Park workers coming to collect the garbage in the afternoon told the news that the man was found. He had a broken leg and suffered from exposure, what with almost freezing temperatures in the night and scorching sun during the day.

Mom took time out from lessons for them to discuss what had happened. The kids knew well the mistakes the man made.

"You're never supposed to go off alone," one of them said.

"And you always check in at a ranger station to let them know where you're going and when you'll be back," said another.

"You take water," one of the twins said.

"And food," his brother chimed in.

"And a flashlight," Belita said, "in case you're out after dark."

"Those are safety precautions, aren't they?" Mom said. "But some people feel that's their private business. What do you think of that?"

"No," Allis said. "When something goes wrong and you need help, how would rescuers know where to find you?"

"Look at the trouble he caused by acting hard-headed," Travis said. "The men who found him risked a lot. They had to haul him up a cliff and pack him out where there wasn't a trail."

"Besides that, they missed two days' work to find him," Belita added.

They agreed the man had done a stupid and dangerous thing, something they would never do.

Before the month was out, they had another misadventure to talk about. A car was found mired in sand drifts on a road posted with signs forbidding park visitors to use it. In the car were a shovel and a pick, and several cactus plants that had been dug.

"I thought everybody knew you can't dig plants in a national park," Page said.

"People are told that when they enter the park," Allis said. "But some of them think they can get away with it."

It turned out that a husband and wife, registered at the lodge, owned the car, but they hadn't been seen since going out one morning for a scenic drive. No trace could be found of the couple. During the search, Mr. Allman dropped by school at morning recess. Everybody gathered round while he talked to Mom and Travis.

"Both these people left the car," he said, "looking for help, we suppose. They won't survive long if we don't find them fast. They're not dressed properly and they don't have food or water, so far as we know. Clete's already tracking one of them, but we need Travis too, because apparently they went in opposite directions."

When Travis got in the car with Mr. Allman, Page saw all evidence of the first grader vanish. Over his face settled a quiet, focused expression. He was listening intently to Mr. Allman as they drove away.

Sam and Lily beamed as proudly as parents. "Not to worry," Sam said, "Travis'll find them."

"He can find whatever's lost," Lily said. "Wait and see."

At three o'clock, nobody wanted to go home without knowing the outcome of the search. However, Mrs. Lawrence came to drive Sam and Lily home in her car, knowing the ranch folks would be worried. Allis hung around school helping Page clean until finally Clete brought Travis back. They both had a weary droop to their shoulders, and dusty boots. Mom invited them in to rest a moment, but Travis declined with thanks. He said he had to get back to the ranch for chores.

"You're excused from homework," Mom said. He gave her a quick shy smile, climbed in the pickup, and took off. Clete agreed to stay, though, and Page and Mom set the table and prepared a quick, light supper while Allis ran across the arroyo to ask permission to join them. Clete washed up in the boys' restroom, and relaxed without talking in the big chair until Allis returned and the food was ready. Page thought the tired lines in his face made him look more hawk-like than usual.

While they ate, he told them what happened, how he followed the man's wandering trail through brush and heat for nearly eleven miles, at last finding him sprawled dead beside a dry creek. Travis tracked the woman, who eventually made her way up into a canyon to a pool of water that had collected in the rocks. She sat down and waited, drinking from the pool, and wetting her face, arms, and shirt in the water to lower her body temperature.

"They paid a big price for those cacti," Mom said.

"Yes," Clete agreed. "The woman said they have a cactus garden in the city. They wanted to add to their collection."

Dark came over Panther Flat while they sat at the table. Through the open windows, Page watched it move toward them from the Dead Horse, soft and secret, beautiful and dangerous, with an underlying chill. It came into this room where they sat warm and safe. She shuddered at the thought of being out in that darkness alone on a parched desert or in a nameless canyon, with no one knowing where she was. At that moment she knew she'd never do anything as foolish as these people had done.

Mom noticed her shudder and arose to turn on the light. That broke the spell. Clete said he should go, and thanked them for such a pleasant ending to a tragic day. Page and Allis cleared the table and did the dishes while Mom worked in the school. Afterward Page and Mom walked Allis home, using the new flashlight they had ordered from Billy Newhouse. On the way back, they heard rustling and chittering sounds in the brush, but neither of them felt curious tonight. They kept their light shining ahead of them on the path.

14

TO PAGE the members of the school board were faceless watchdogs, except for Mr. Allman. She thought of him as "President," with a capital "P," but she did not know the members he was president of until the board held a meeting at the school. Page was out back, finishing with her chores, when Clete drove onto the playground in his white pickup. She felt shy around this strange, quiet man who could do everything so well. He was like a legendary character from the Big Bend book who used his fiddle to talk for him. He walked toward where she stood on the porch holding the mop. Again she noted his catlike movements, and how his feet made no sound on the gravel.

She had thought a lot about him since the night he ate supper with them. She knew he worked for the border patrol, which Page imagined was something like the Texas Rangers. The kids had told her he lived alone in a ghost town near the river, a town that used to be an important quicksilver producing center. Some of them had brought to school cinnabar ore from Clete's, a rosy red ore the color of the Rosillas Mountains at sunset. Page had examined it and pondered over it. How could this dried-up ore produce the liquid mercury that took on such life when it spilled? She remembered the time she broke Dad's thermometer, how the droplets of quicksilver scattered across the floor. They had been uncatchable!

She wished she could know Clete better, but now that she had the chance her tongue felt tied in a knot.

He said, "I heard you and Allis want to find the treasure of the Chisos."

Startled, she said, "How could you hear that? Who told you?"

The smile that flashed across his tan face softened the hawk-like profile. "Maybe a spirit of the Chisos."

Was he making fun of her and Allis? "We know where the treasure is," she bragged.

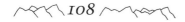

"How is that?"

Laying aside the mop, she wiped her hands on her shirt, intending to bring the legend book out of its hiding place in the supply closet. Questions stopped her: Could he be trusted? Might he tell Mom, or some of the others, about their treasure-hunting plans? Would they make fun of her and Allis? Or if the treasure were really there where she and Allis believed, would he take their carefully thought out clues and find it himself? She looked at him warily. "We've found lots of different treasure stories."

"Which one do you accept?"

She refused to fall into the trap of pinpointing the one they chose. "The story we've found most often," she answered truthfully, "is about the old Spanish mission down on the river. Do you know it?"

He nodded. "You stand in the chapel door Easter morning and watch for the first rays of the rising sun to strike the Chisos. That shows you the treasure cave."

"Neat, isn't it? But we can't wait till Easter." She thought of Dad, and her intention to surprise him with the gold. "We're going to search now."

She heard a car approaching. Mrs. Lawrence drove onto the playground and parked beside Clete's pickup. Was she a board member too?

"Those stories are interesting," Clete said. "But don't take them too seriously. Above all, don't do anything reckless."

"Like what?" Page asked.

"Like going into the mountains alone."

She knew he spoke with authority, but she felt

a little miffed that he thought she needed advice. "Oh, we won't be that stupid," she said.

Mrs. Lawrence greeted them with a smile. "I drove over," she said, "because I thought I was late." Soon Mr. Allman strode up and together the board went inside to meet with Mom. Clete held the door for the others to precede him. Looking back at Page he said, "Don't go into the Chisos alone." It seemed almost an order. She didn't acknowledge it.

Page finished with her work. Rather than traipse through the school and interrupt the meeting she walked around, past the water pan, to the front patio. She sat a while there watching night come, and thinking about Clete. The boys adored him. He played the fiddle with verve. He knew the ways of the wilderness, and he rescued people. Now she'd found out he served on the school board. All of that meant he could be trusted, didn't it? He seemed to think the treasure a joke, yet he spoke his warning seriously. She knew he was thinking of the people who'd gotten in trouble recently. But she and Allis used good judgment. They were Big Benders too. That made her smile. She'd never thought of herself before as a Big Bender. What was happening to her?

She recognized something else happening to her tonight, this minute—a change in the way she thought of the board. Before, they were like a fearsome, three-headed blob that could fire Mom and send Page away. Now they were people she knew— Doug's dad, Allis's mother, and Clete who could fiddle the stars out of the sky, as she'd heard somebody say.

But secretly she thought of him as the Comanche. She wondered what they were meeting about tonight.

She went to the kitchen area and made a sandwich to eat while doing her homework. The murmuring voices from the schoolroom provided background sound for her studies. About nine o'clock the voices raised in "good nights," the outside door opened and shut, and motors growled to life. The meeting had ended, yet Mom didn't come into the apartment immediately. When she did, Page could see she was wilted and unhappy. She kicked off her shoes and sank into the big chair.

"I suppose I shouldn't be surprised," she said. "The Boatwrights and the Hills are complaining that I'm not teaching the basics. Bret and Bart's parents support them."

"The twins sure love school," Page tried to comfort her. "They come early and stay late."

"Yes. And they both have kept exceptional journals on their solar observations. But these parents claim that if they're transferred, the students will be behind in their studies."

"How do they want you to teach?"

"They want the day divided into periods—math, reading, spelling, grammar, health, penmanship. Cut and dried, cover the material in the textbook, then take up another book. No social studies, no science, no journal writing, no projects like the solar system mobile."

"But that's what makes school fun!"

"They say it's all right to have a film once in a

while." She rubbed her scalp as if her head ached. "The board supports my way of teaching. They say it's exactly what they visualized when they hired me. But they have to appease the others somehow. Or I guess it's I who have to appease them."

After that, Page noted changes Mom made in her teaching. Instead of searching for information through all the many books Mom had collected for them, the students had to follow the textbooks page by page. Seldom did they have time for an exciting discussion where they shared knowledge gained, compared notes, disagreed, and provided proof for their points. There wasn't enough time for working on the magazine they had begun putting together to summarize the solar system unit, or doing any art work. Page saw that Mom tried hard to do what the dissatisfied parents wanted, even though it contradicted what she thought was good schooling. That showed her how much Mom longed to be accepted in the Big Bend, and to have a future here.

Later that week, Gypsy Meg burst in during school, long red skirt swishing and bracelets jangling. Margaret looked at her with pride as she strode over to Mom and demanded, "What's this I hear about certain goings-on?"

Mom hastily invited her into the apartment, leaving the door open so the students understood they should continue with their work. Page could hear their voices, accompanied by the rattle of coffee cups in the saucers. Gypsy Meg spoke with strong feeling, Mom low and soft.

Afterwards, Mom seemed more cheerful than she'd been lately.

An ally, thought Page. Gypsy Meg will be a good one, a fighting one.

Later Page found out she'd been right. Gypsy Meg had come to declare herself on Mom's side.

"Aren't you glad?" Page asked.

"In a way, yes," Mom said, "but Meg wants a showdown with the other side. That would polarize the community in the worst way."

"All-out war?" Page said, grinning. If the situation came to that point she could make her accusations against Mack Hill and Hank Boatwright. "Vengeance for Victorio!" That would be her battle cry. Doug would be the first one she'd tell. He was a solemn boy before the tragedy, but since then there was a sorrowfulness about him that worried her.

Mom said in her laying-down-the-law tone, "We can't have all-out war. It would destroy the school."

After Page thought everything over, she realized Mom was right. For a short while, Page would glory in revenge on the boys. But living here, and having the school, was an everyday, long-term kind of thing. She would have to continue to hold her tongue and let Mom work the problem out her way.

15

DURING PLAY PERIOD, Page and Allis liked to pore over the legend book in the shade of the porch, using the magnifying glass Billy Newhouse sent to the school. With it they deciphered one set of handwriting which was English. Another writing seemed to be in Spanish. With high hopes they showed the notations to Travis who stared at them blankly. He spoke such fluent Spanish they'd never realized till that moment that he couldn't read it. They were embarrassed, but Travis said with firm decision, "I can't read it now, but I will some day."

He was natural and unashamed, which helped Page recover quickly. Here was a chance to find out something she wondered about. "Why can't you read?" She knew it was not because he lacked intelligence. Often as Mom looked over the day's schoolwork she commented on Travis's rapid progress.

He said without self-pity, "You know how big this county is? Bigger than some states. You know how many schools we had in this county? One, up in the mountains. Too far for me to walk and work the ranch too. Now I'm sixteen and can drive, got to make up for lost time."

"But aren't there other kids on ranches? What do they do?"

"Their moms live with them in town during the week," Allis said. "The really rich ranch kids have governesses, and private planes."

"Bet they don't have as much fun as we do," Margaret said.

The students of the Panther Flat school did have fun and were always thinking up something interesting to do. Page's favorite was the bullfight. Little, dark Jesús was the fierce bull for Epifanio's matador, pawing and bellowing and tossing his head. Epifanio kept a muleta in the supply closet—a red flag which was

nailed to a stick—to taunt the bull and enrage him. The wooden sword, which Epifanio carved and painted—the blade silver, the hilt ornately gold— he kept in his desk.

"See, this is black velvet," Epifanio would shout to the spectators, indicating his jacket and his pants. "And this," he poufed out his shirt at the neck, "is lace. Along the sleeves are jewels, and I am being paid fifty thousand dollars for this fight." Sometimes the bull was not cooperative. He was not always willing to be killed, nor to have his ears cut off to be presented to the matador. Before one fight, Jesús emerged from the boys' bathroom with his black hair a mass of white soapsuds that he had sculpted into two slightly lopsided horns. Everybody clapped and cheered, gathering round the circle drawn in the playground dirt to mark the bullring. Even Mom came to watch that fight, bringing small pieces of colored paper, which the kids crumpled for flowers to toss at the bull as well as the matador.

With so much else occupying her mind, Page had forgotten her determination to discover how to tell Bret and Bart apart. It came back to her the day she realized that Mom knew.

"Bret," Mom said, "please bring me your journal." As she spoke, she looked at one of the boys. He did not look up, but his brother across the room started toward her, notebook in hand. Mom continued looking at the seated twin. "Bret," she repeated firmly, "I need to see your astronomy journal."

The boys knew their charade was up. The other brother returned to his desk, and the seated brother sheepishly rose and took his notebook to her.

Page fixed in her mind where Bret's desk stood. The trouble was the boys swapped places freely when no one was watching. But next time Mom spoke to a twin she called him correctly again. Mom knew their secret! Page could hardly wait till after school to find out.

But Mom refused to tell her. "That'll take the fun out of identifying them for you," she laughed. "You know that there is a way—keep watching for it."

Page sulked and complained to Allis. "I've got to figure them out."

Allis shrugged and said, "I don't call them, so it's no problem for me." She was more worried about the possibility that her father would be transferred from the Big Bend. Her mother had cautioned her about getting too fond of Page. "I know what that means," Allis told Page. "Next, she'll say to your mother that maybe we shouldn't spend so much time together, that saying good-bye will be too hard. I've been through this before."

"But you can't leave! We haven't explored the canyon yet! I won't let you go!"

They both laughed at that impossible statement. Quickly they turned serious, trying to think of someone who would go into the canyon with them. Before long, school would be out for Christmas holidays. They hadn't found anyone who was willing, or who had time, or who thought the hike into the canyon would be worthwhile. They were so desperate they asked Allis' mother if she'd go with them.

"Why do you want to go back into Panther Peak? That's so wild and rough," was her reaction. "Why not take Lost Mine where the trail is easier?"

"Everybody goes up Lost Mine," Allis said. She and Page silently agreed that if a treasure had ever been there, somebody had already found it.

Mrs. Lawrence wouldn't change her mind. Page and Allis suspected a conspiracy among the adults to keep them from going but didn't know what to do about it. However, when Mr. Lawrence received word he would be transferred in January to a national park in faraway Maine the friends made a desperate decision.

"It's up to you and me to find the treasure," Allis said.

"We can't wait for anybody else," Page agreed.

They began preparations right away. Already they knew by heart what the legend book had to say about the Panther Peak canyon. The very shape of it seemed to be a portent of good fortune—a horseshoe, and with a double entrance. What could be unsafe about that?

Each time they talked it over, their decision to go seemed the only choice they had. They would take a look into the canyon, they agreed. If it appeared too dangerous, they would turn back and no one need know. The only catch was that if they found the treasure, their parents would know they had disobeyed. But would it matter then? Gold bars! How could they bring them out? They planned to scuttle their equipment, and each one take as many bars as she could in her backpack.

They started out in the direction of Comanche Butte early on a Saturday when Page's mom was especially busy. They didn't say that the Butte was their destination. Allis only said that they were going arrowhead hunting. When Mom asked where they planned to go, Page waved vaguely toward Comanche Butte and the Chisos Mountains. Her mother, working on an order for films Clete had agreed to pick up on his way to town, didn't glance at them. "Be careful," she said.

Page felt guilty that Mom trusted them without question. But she soon forgot as they began working out the plan they'd dreamed about for so long. They walked toward the Butte until the school dropped from sight, then they veered right and headed for the Chisos. Once they started climbing, the school came back into view, and all of the Panther Flat settlement. A white pickup stood parked at the school door, and Page could see Clete getting out, glancing around in his alert, all-seeing way. Knowing well that they would be visible to him—especially Allis who wore a red shirt—they kept themselves concealed by foliage as much as possible until the mountain closed around them. They sighted a rock formation, high to their left, a stack of huge boulders topped by an enormous mushroom cap of stone that appeared to teeter on the edge of an abyss.

"That can be our landmark," said Allis. They headed up the precipitous, tangled cliff side toward it, scattering rocks as they struggled.

"I know why we never see javelinas or panthers when we're hiking. We make too much noise," Page grumbled. "But there's no way to be quiet if you move at all."

Once she looked down. The stones rolled at top-speed from under her feet and plunged to the desert flat far below. Quickly, she averted her eyes to the landmark gradually looming closer to them, almost chalk white against the cloudless blue sky. She thought she could never reach it, but Allis forged ahead through brush and thorns, and Page forced herself to follow.

At the top they sank down in the shadow of the rock formation, removing their caps, wiping their faces, and unscrewing their canteens. Page was so glad to find coolness that she didn't give a nervous thought to the massive rock balanced above their heads that provided the shade. An unspoken agreement, something Page had learned good friends could have, kept them facing the way they had come up, with their backs to whatever waited for them. After cooling down, and beginning to breathe normally again, their eyes met in suspense.

"Ready?" Page asked.

Allis nodded. "Remember, if it's too wild and dangerous, we'll go back."

Without rising they turned themselves one-hundred-eighty degrees and looked down into a canyon that fitted the words "wild and dangerous" more exactly than any they'd ever seen. However, it was so beautiful they instantly forgot the sensible decision they had made about turning back. Page marveled to see the canyon sides that looked like castle turrets colored with the delicate shades of lavender, rose, blue, and cream. And in the depths of the canyon, what rich greens! The pine trees below were ancient giants, and the breeze wafted upward the warm clean smell of their smoky green needles.

"Must be a stream down there," Allis murmured. "Everything's green and fresh."

Page took a deep breath, filling her lungs with the fragrant air. "Let's go!"

The way to the bottom was even rougher than it looked. They made faster progress when they could sit and slide. Once down they agreed they'd never seen any place so lovely. The thick pine needles formed the softest, finest carpet underfoot, and the stream, though small, was clear and frolicking, with ferns along the edges. After walking a while they chose a place for lunch, leaning against a great rock so untouched by sun it cooled them through their shirts. They talked little while they ate, listening to the calls of a canyon wren amplified by the sheer walls of the canyon. The music of the stream tempted Page to stretch out on the bright brown straw for a *siesta*. Allis brought her to her feet with the reminder that time would not hold still for them. Page took a moment to put her arm around a big tree to steady herself while looking up, up to where a slit of blue sky showed between canyon walls. Then they hurried along, following the stream toward what they hoped was the treasure cave beside the hundred-foot drop-off. Sometimes the shade was so deep Page glanced again to the blue far overhead for reassurance that day was still there.

During a pause while they drained the last of the water from their canteens, Page suddenly realized the canyon was leading them away from Panther Peak. Before long Allis, with a troubled frown, confirmed her suspicions. "Something's wrong. We ought to be going the other direction—I think."

While they stood silent, wondering what to do, Page felt a tremor that came up through her shoe-soles and shook her body. Far off, a low growling swelled and rolled toward them.

Allis' eyes widened. "A storm! Somewhere. That means rain, and the canyon may flood." She whirled to the straight-up wall and began climbing. "Hurry! If we can find a shelf up there . . . ," she strained her neck back, searching the walls, "we'll be all right."

Page went after her, seizing bushes, thorns, anything that would help lever her up from the canyon floor. The wind swooped down, rocking the big pines, making them shriek in a humanlike voice. Where could she hide? She longed to crawl under a rock or into a crack where she could cover her head and not see or hear the fury around them. But she knew they must not be caught on the canyon floor with a flood on the way. She scrambled straight up after Allis.

Then the lightning began zapping down, each flash followed by a frying sound and a crash of thunder, which the canyon trapped and tossed from wall to wall. Page had never heard such thunder that rumbled on and on, then started over again. Before the booming echoes faded downstream, the next flash came. Page had never seen such lightening, dead white and almost too quick for the eye to see. She did not want to climb closer to it, but the thought of a wall of water roaring down upon her, sweeping her toward the drop-off was worse.

With a rush the wind drove the rain upon them so hard the first drops felt like hail stones. It blinded Page as she clung to the canyon-side, not wanting to go up, fearing to go down. Allis reached a hand to her and shouted, "Hurry!"

As she drew herself up even with Allis, clinging to a bush, Page panted, "Where can we hide—there must be a place—"

Allis, peering right and left through the rain, exclaimed, "An overhang! Come on!"

Page could see no place of safety, but she struggled to follow her friend. Allis had found a rock ledge jutting from the cliff with enough space underneath for them to huddle. The noise all around deafened Page,

and watching the giant trees thrashing helplessly in the wind filled her with terror.

"We're high enough here," Allis shouted against her ear, above a new steady roar that was neither wind nor thunder. She pointed up-canyon, toward the way they had come. A boiling wall of water churned toward them swallowing the merry little stream, bulldozing boulders and logs, drowning their picnic spot. The power of this raging river as it poured past far below them matched the awesome lightning, the thunder, and the wind. The terrifying combination drove Page back under the ledge, pressing hard against a stunted bush growing from the rock. The sharp limbs felt like knives, but Page didn't care. She wanted to burrow as far back into the mountain as she could go. No bush could stand in her way. The crackling limbs gave way catapulting Page backward. She grabbed for Allis as she fell, dragging her down too.

Flashes of lightning showed the bush had concealed a jagged split in the rocks. Without pausing to see if they were hurt, Page shouted, "In here! Quick!" Turning sideways they squeezed through the crack and crouched close to the ground. The storm intensified; lightning seemed to reach in for them. They held hands tightly without talking.

Page suspected that Allis was thinking thoughts similar to hers, remembering the foolish people who went out ill equipped without telling anyone their destination. Her own vow that day in school echoed in her mind: "I would never be that stupid!" And she had ignored Clete's warning, "Don't go into the Chisos alone." How could she and Allis have done this terrible thing? If they died here in this hidden place, nobody would ever find them. She pictured Mom watching for them to return from their hike. How puzzled she would be, then how worried and sad. Page hid her face on her drawn up knees, making her mind a blank.

When the storm finally released the canyon from its fury, an intense quiet remained. The girls sat as if in a trance until the call of a canyon wren, loud and clear, brought them to life. The sun shone with renewed brightness reflecting light into their hiding place through the crack in the rocks.

Allis stood with difficulty, looking around. "Whew! Where are we?"

"A hidden cave," Page said with awe. "No bigger than our apartment. Could this be . . . ?" In the dimness they could see this was a pocket of safety, of refuge. There were no goatskins of gold nuggets, no stacked gold bars, but on a rock shelf at the rear, Page picked up what appeared to be a fragment of a sandal.

"The basket weavers," Allis said, touching it with reverence. "Old, old. Look at the pattern, how beautiful. They used threads from the century plant."

"I remember," said Page softly. "During the Mexico Moon they had to hide to save themselves from the Comanches."

"But finally they were all killed, or driven away from the Big Bend."

"Dare I take it?" Page asked, standing irresolute, holding the fiber weaving that had in an instant become more valuable to her than gold bars.

Allis said nothing, waiting.

Page, after a moment, laid the weaving back on the ledge, in the exact spot she'd found it. Maybe hundreds of years from now somebody else would squeeze through the split into this cave. They might pick up this beautiful weaving that not only had the cave dwellers' fingerprints on it, but now her own. She followed Allis sidewise through the crack to stand once again on the narrow space under the ledge.

Down below, the stream was still swollen but moving with less force. Blocking its way were the huge boulders the flood had brought and a giant pine that had given way before the storm.

"It's late. We've got to speed," Allis said. "Wish I knew a short cut."

Page thought how wildly foolish it was for Allis to talk about speed when now they were hampered not only by the rough terrain and steep climb, but the ground turned to wet glass by the rain. She wouldn't allow herself to think of how upset and worried Mom and the Lawrences must be at this moment, concentrating instead on the struggle upward. Her desperate hope was that once they reached the canyon rim they could see the tablerock landmark.

Above her, Allis gasped and froze. Page looked up to see her stone-still, white and staring. With failing heart she followed her gaze to see a figure moving silently and easily down from the rim. A man in rough clothes the color of the desert, his skin dark and long hair black as charcoal, raised his face to them. Black eyes, a hook nose, high cheek bones and a strong jaw marked him as a Comanche of the first rank. No slave Indian ghost was this, nor peaceful basket weaver.

The fright that wracked Page at that moment blinded her to common sense. Confrontation with an all-too-human Ghost of the Chisos rendered her helpless. She couldn't even scream, though that was what she most wanted to do.

The man raised his hand, and a white smile softened his fierce features. He called, "Allis! Page! I've come for you."

"Clete!" Allis whispered.

Weak with relief, Page could not move, neither could Allis. They stood where they were, watching, while he came nearer.

His keen eyes looked them over. "Are you all right?"

"Yes. But how—" Allis stuttered.

"How did you find us?" Page grasped his hand in gladness, and Allis hugged him.

"You remember, I warned you about coming here?" He looked at Page. She nodded. "I knew you did not accept that warning, that you still meant to come. I was at the school this morning when your mother told me you had gone to Comanche Butte. But even as she said it, I saw two figures, one in a red shirt, going along the side of old Panther. What could that mean?"

Page remembered that moment near the beginning of the hike when they'd looked at the panorama of Panther Flat. She had seen Clete arrive at the school to pick up the list of films from Mom, and knew they should conceal themselves in a hurry. How glad she was he hadn't missed seeing them!

He took a candy bar from his pocket and opened his canteen. "Sit here to rest for *un momentito.*"

Allis glanced anxiously at the distance between them and the rim. "Our moms—we should go—they'll be worried sick."

"Yes. They already are. But you are too tired now."

They sank down in the brush, taking turns with the canteen, and munching the candy. Page could hardly raise the canteen to drink. "But how did you know where to come?" she asked.

"When I returned from town to deliver the films, you still had not come home. Your mother was concerned. Mrs. Lawrence came. She too was worried, especially when we saw the storm over the Chisos." He sat on a rock near them, mud caked on his boots. "I know these mountains from a long time back. There is one canyon that you cannot miss getting into when you enter the Chisos from the point where you were. This is so because of that one particular balanced rock. A shortcut came back to my mind. I brought my truck for you. It's just across that arroyo and over the next spur, parked on the lodge road."

"The lodge road?" Page said, unbelieving.

"Yes," he said, smiling again, though Page never felt that he was laughing at them. "You two walked many horizontal miles today, besides the vertical miles."

After a few more minutes of rest and recovery, they started for Clete's pickup. What a great moment when they climbed in, the engine clanked to life, and the wheels began rolling down the rain-slick lodge road toward Panther Flat.

16

THEIR PARENTS WERE SO RELIEVED to have them back unhurt that the girls thought punishment might be forgotten. It wasn't. Mom and the Lawrences decided they should do community service, which in this case meant scrubbing the schoolroom floor and cleaning and polishing the schoolhouse windows, especially the long east wall from floor to ceiling. When Page and Allis compared notes they found that Allis had orthodontist appointments on some Saturdays when Page was free, and Page and Mom had errands in town or invitations to visit outlying ranches when Allis was free. They decided what equipment they would need and made plans to meet on the only Saturday when both of them could work together. They intended to do the floor first, then while it dried they would wash the windows, with one girl working on the inside while the other washed outside on the same window. That way they could do a cleaner job and do it faster, they figured. Mr. Lawrence agreed that on the morning of their work day he would bring over some men to move all the desks and chairs out on the porch. The rest of the job was up to Allis and Page.

As the day drew nearer the girls were dismayed to

learn that Gypsy Meg's annual barbecue was set for that Saturday too.

"Let's see if we can postpone our sentence," Allis said.

"Let's. I've never seen the river, nor Carmencita."

Their parents considered the request, but since there was no other time the girls could do the work until after the Christmas holidays, they decided not to allow a change.

"You committed a serious offense," Mr. Lawrence said. "I don't think the punishment should be delayed."

Mom and Mrs. Lawrence agreed. So on that gold and blue December day Page and Allis sat on the edge of the patio surrounded by their work equipment— clean rags, newspapers, window cleaner, a ladder and a step stool. They saw every vehicle in Panther Flat pull away, leaving them behind. They watched the stream of traffic on the distant river road headed for Gypsy Meg's. When the traffic flow dried up to only a tourist car now and then going toward the Chisos, they realized they were alone. They were the only park residents not at the barbecue except for the few personnel who had to work. They felt abandoned and gave way to self-pity for awhile.

"I sure wanted to see a tame panther," Page complained.

"I wanted to eat!" Allis threw a rock toward the arroyo. "Gypsy Meg has the best food—barbecue and everything that goes with it. I'm hungry just thinking about it."

They decided to go inside and fix snacks. After that

they leafed through some magazines but found nothing interesting.

Page yawned. "Might as well get started."

"Okay," Allis sighed.

Without furniture the schoolroom looked bizarre, and Page was sure the cement floor was bigger than a football field. They tackled the job in three stages: scrubbing with a stiff broom and hot soapy water; mopping up the dirty water; then rinsing with buckets of clear water. They couldn't think of an easier way, and it was hot, sweaty work.

"This is filthy," Allis said, wringing out the mop. "Don't you sweep it every day after school?" Her voice sounded a little cross.

"Yeah, but you know how the dust blows in. And when it rains nobody cleans off their boots." Page felt kind of cross too. "And I'm getting blisters on my hands. Let's take a break."

They were resting on the patio when they saw Clete's white pickup coming from riverward. He turned on the Panther Flat road, then onto the school road.

"He's coming here!" Allis jumped up.

"Oh! Wonder why?"

They ran to the back of the school where he was parking.

"Big Bend can't have *la fiesta* without its two bravest adventurers," Clete said, getting out in that smooth, quiet way that he had and rolling up his white sleeves. He reached in back of the truck. "I have permission to serve as a consultant on this cleaning job, as long as I don't touch a floor or a window. Is that all right?"

"Yes!" they said together, taking the jugs and containers he handed them.

How proud they were to show him they had already finished the floor. With the doors propped open it was rapidly drying.

"Good job. You've done the hardest part," he said.

"You'll make quick work of the windows. Here's how." He directed them to make up a can of sudsy ammonia water, then each take a mop, dip it in the suds, and scrub the windows from top to bottom. He followed along with a wide squeegee, a rubber scraper on the end of a long handle, which he dragged down the windows, drying them off.

"You observe," he said smiling, "that I'm not touching a window."

No climbing up and down ladders nor standing on step stools. No polishing the glass with newspapers. In a short time the chore was done, leaving the windows so clean they were invisible.

"Suppose we throw in a bonus," Clete suggested. "Wash the teacher's windows too." They tackled the large windows of the apartment plus the smaller one in the bathroom, and the glass door that opened onto the patio. Standing away from the building, surveying the results of their work, Page felt pleased.

"Another good job," Clete said. Then he looked at the sun and added, "Time to go. The barbecue will be ready for eating *pronto.*"

They put away the equipment, Clete's in his truck and the rest in the school supply closet. He waited while they made themselves neat, then off they went toward the river.

The scenery changed almost immediately, Page noticed. The narrow road began a gradual descent, curving through hills and buttes more weird than she'd seen elsewhere in the park. Clete concentrated on the driving, while Allis overflowed with information about points of interest.

"That's the road to Glen Springs," she pointed out as they passed what looked like desert with faint tire tracks. "Pancho Villa's men raided Glen Springs. They killed Gypsy Meg's husband."

"Oh," said Page startled. "Why did they come here? Gypsy Meg and her husband, I mean."

"They homesteaded on the river, where we're going now. Afterwards Gypsy Meg stayed on."

Page couldn't always follow Allis's comments, or recognize what she was talking about. One figure she could see with no mistake was an enormous rock eroded into a rattlesnake with its mouth open—even the fangs showed. "You can stand in its mouth and I'll take your picture," Allis teased.

"No, thanks," Page muttered, looking down into a deep canyon bordering the road. "What if we met somebody on this road?"

"There're two roads," Allis said. "One to go there and another to come back."

The rose-striped Sierra del Carmens loomed ever more immense, shutting out the sky. At their base, winding lazily along through barren stretches of dun earth, green canebrakes, and willows that had turned a brilliant yellow, was the Rio Grande. Page caught her breath at the first glimpse of it. Beyond, she could see a huddle of adobe houses, and several burros, one of them a pinto.

Mexico!

Nothing but the river's width separated them from this mysterious foreign country. She wriggled with excitement. "Oh, thank you, Clete, for coming for us! I didn't want to miss this party."

"Me either," Allis chimed in. "And there it is!"

Below them, as they made the last descent to river level, stood an earth-colored house with a long porch roofed in dried stalks of river cane. People gathered in its shade, some sitting, some standing, while others scattered in groups between the house and the river. Up close, Page was surprised to see how large the house was. From a distance it had been dwarfed by the great mountain range across the river and the high rough bluffs rising behind it. River canes with fuzzy tops, shocked like corn, decorated the bare yard, while desert plants of various green shades grew against the house, seeming to secure it to the hard earth. Two long tables in the shade of tamarisk trees were spread with food, while a third table, centered with a ten gallon glass jug filled with fluffy cane tops, stood vacant.

"That's for the barbecue," Allis said. A long brightly colored banner rippled from the porch, welcoming everybody in English and Spanish.

Margaret ran toward them through the crowd, and seized their hands. "Come see the barbecue pit! They're bringing up the meat now."

The pit was like a deep round well. Down in the bottom Page could see bundles wrapped in steaming cloths and resting on racks.

"That's the meat," Margaret said. "Smell it? Yummm. Goat—*cabrito*—and beef. It's been cooking since last night."

The odor was delicious, but heat and steam from the pit made Page flinch. The man in charge of the cooking had his helpers bringing up the bundles, one at a time. He slit the wrapping of each bundle. Steam gushed out, and there was the meat, so tender it fell away from the bones.

As soon as the men arranged the barbecue on platters, it was carried to the center table. The other tables, crowded with dishes of Mexican food, smelled like peppers, cornmeal, and beans. Some of the kids crowded around big tubs where bottles of soda pop nestled in crushed ice. Page, Allis, and Margaret, however, decided to start with the barbecue, then work their way around to the other tables and leave the drinks for last. Along the way, Page saw Mom and thanked her for letting Clete come for them.

"I didn't want you to miss this," Mom said, her eyes shining. She wore a yellow dress, and looked as radiant as the Rio Grande willows in the sunlight. Gypsy Meg, swaying from group to group, talked louder and laughed longer than anyone.

Margaret led Allis and Page to a pile of boulders under the willows where they settled with their heaped-up plates. They could listen to the water rippling past while they ate and watched the crowd. They saw most of their classmates, either walking with their families, or playing at the river's edge. Tied to a hitching rail in the shade were several burros, fitted with saddles, bridles, and stirrups. Page thought that the heavy gear made them look overloaded.

"Want to ride across the river?" Margaret asked as they dumped their trash in a big box.

"Sure!" Page was surprised. "But they look so small, and I'm so big."

"Silly! They carry full-grown men and big heavy loads. Burros are strong."

That might be true, but they certainly didn't look eager to go. They stood asleep, with one hind leg relaxed, ears drooping, eyes closed, their soft gray muzzles gently moving when they breathed. It was almost as if they hoped no one would notice them.

Page couldn't resist riding one. She'd never even been on a mule or horse. She mounted easily enough, but couldn't persuade the burro to move. No matter what she said or did, he locked his small hooves in place and refused to budge. Allis trotted away, but in the wrong direction. Margaret headed for the river, screaming over her shoulder to follow her. "Show him you're boss!" she shouted.

Finally Page dismounted, and tried to lead the burro. He balked at leading, too. Other kids, gathering to watch, called out advice. "Kick him!" somebody yelled. "Make him go!" Page felt she had hurt the animal enough already, jerking on the reins which pulled the bit against his mouth. Finally she suggested to the kids that she would mount again and nudge the burro with her heels while they pushed him from behind to get him started toward Mexico. That made them laugh, loud and long.

"No way!" Doug said. "Nobody'll risk getting kicked by a burro."

By this time, Margaret was almost across the river, and Allis had her burro ready to step in the water. Page had to get hers going! She wanted at least to stand on Mexican ground today. She dropped the reins and ran to the nearest table where she chose carrots to tempt him. At the last minute, feeling foolish, she grabbed a couple of tortillas and ran back to the hitching rail.

The burro was sleeping again. She shouted at him and pulled on his ear, which somebody said was how you got a burro's attention. His eyes opened. He rubbed his soft muzzle over the carrots, but didn't bite them. She offered the tortillas. That was what he wanted! He wrapped his velvety lips around the whole tortilla, almost inhaling it. Remounting, she got him started while he was distracted by his enjoyment of the tortilla. Each time he faltered, she kicked him for fear he'd stop again.

Allis and her burro were now mid-river, with the

water halfway up his legs. The burro had decided to lie down, and Allis was frantically pulling the reins and kicking his sides to change his mind. Now Page's burro struck a brisk trot into the river and surefootedly waded across, passing Allis, whom Margaret had returned to rescue. All three girls ended up in Mexico with their burros, but they were so tired from the struggle they sat a while in the sand before attempting the return trip.

"I'm glad I brought an extra tortilla," Page said. "In case they refuse to take us back to the U.S."

She divided the tortilla in thirds, one for each donkey. After Page and Allis mounted, Margaret lured their donkeys to the riverbank by feeding them bits of tortilla. Once they stepped into the water she whacked each donkey on the hindquarters with her open hand, at the same time giving such a raucous yell the animals shot off, switching their tails from side to side fast as they could. The burros didn't stop till they reached the home side. Margaret was close behind.

"That's enough for me," Page said, hitching her mount to the rail. "I had to work harder than he did." The burro sighed deeply and fell asleep.

Shadows grew longer as the sun dropped down toward the bluffs. A Mexican band, in black sombreros and black chaps, appeared with their guitars. They began singing their sad songs in Spanish that drowned out the rush of the Rio Grande over the rapids and the braying of wild burros across in Mexico.

Page jumped up. "Those songs make me want to cry! Let's go somewhere else—do something."

"Carmencita!" said Margaret. "Come on. She's shut in her cage because of the little kids. Carmencita doesn't like little kids."

Carmencita's relaxed tan body lay along one side of the strong cage, her head turned away from them toward the river. Only the black tip of her handsome tan tail moved, back and forth, in a thoughtful rhythm.

"She's meditating," Margaret whispered. "I never interrupt her when she's meditating."

"How did your grandma get her?" Page asked.

"A man brought her from Mexico. She was an orphan, so tiny her eyes weren't open. And she was spotted." Her whispered laugh sounded breathy. "Looking at her now you can't believe that."

"Doesn't she get lonely for other panthers?" Allis asked.

"Maybe for her brother, but he died before the man brought Carmencita here. He walked a long way to bring her to Grandma 'cause he knew she could make Carmencita live."

They stood quietly watching the puma. Page willed her to turn that aloof head and look at them, but she never did.

"She knows we're here," Margaret said. "But she doesn't like for Grandma to have parties. She wants just people she knows to be around her."

The visit to Carmencita was very unsatisfying to Page. "If only I could touch her."

"You can come back," Margaret reassured her.

"I won't see her again," Allis sighed. "I'll not be back before we leave, I know."

"That's all right," Margaret said seriously. "Where

you're going you'll probably see baby moose. Think of that!"

They tiptoed away, though Page believed no amount of noise would make Carmencita notice anybody if she didn't want to.

The party went on and on. The moon came up, and the sorrowful Spanish songs echoed against the bluffs. The girls made another go-round of the tables, with Page collecting enough tortillas for each burro, still tied to the rail, to have one. She had to awaken them, but they ate with gusto, then fell asleep again.

"They had a hard day," Margaret said. "Before you came, all the little kids were riding them."

Lighted lanterns were set on the tables and hung from posts. The wind rose, blowing from the south, bringing exotic odors of spices and flowers, and rattling the river canes. About midnight, people began gathering their children and saying good-bye. Page and Allis thanked Clete again before getting into the Lawrence car. The last Page heard as they drove away was the saddest of the sad songs, *"Adios,* Margarita," except she substituted "Allisita."

Before school let out for the holidays, Mom gave what she called a comprehensive exam to all grades. She explained that she wanted it to be a review of the year's work thus far, to help fix what they'd learned in their minds before the long holiday. But also, she said, it would help her judge how well she was teaching them. To the upper grades she gave an extra question, one that took them by surprise. She told them they could use any of the resources in the room to find the answer—books, the calendars they had made, the almanac, their heavenly journals. They could even work together.

The question: "A story you've all heard says that on Easter morning if you stand in the door of the Spanish chapel on the river, the first rays of the rising sun will show you where to find the lost treasure in the Chisos. Use what you learned in our solar system unit to prove this story untrue."

At first they were indignant.

"It IS true!" Mack Hill insisted. "An old man in Mexico told me it's true, and he's a hundred years old."

"Sure," Hank Boatwright agreed. "Everybody knows it's true."

Page felt as if Mom had hit her. She and Allis believed the story wholeheartedly. Hadn't they seen it in print? Hadn't they risked their lives for the treasure? Where were any facts disproving it? What did Mom mean?

After finishing with the main part of the exam the older students gathered at the library table, searching through books, rereading their journals, studying the charts and calendars posted around the room.

Belita was the only one not grumbling. She seemed to accept that the story wasn't true and directed all her effort into searching for the proof. She worked steadily and silently until the afternoon when she asked Mom, "Does the answer have to do with the seasons of the year?"

"Yes," said Mom. "When does Easter come?"

"In the spring," Belita said.

"When in the spring?" Mom asked. Everybody was listening now.

"Sunday," someone said.

"But what date?" Mom said.

They didn't answer, but spread out the calendars they had made and opened the almanac to calendars for many years back and many years ahead. By this time, all complaints had stopped. They were like hounds on a scent or a detective looking for clues.

"Easter doesn't come on the same date every year," Belita said.

"Listen," Allis said. "This book says that Easter comes on the first Sunday after the first full moon of spring."

"Here's a year," one of the twins said, "when Easter fell on March 22."

"But look!" his brother added. "On this other calendar Easter is on April 25—a whole month's difference."

"What is the earth doing during that month? Will it be in the same position April 25 as it was March 22?" Mom asked.

"It's revolving around the sun."

"It's changing its position in relation to the sun."

"Days are getting longer."

"The sun looks to be far to the south when spring begins. Then it seems to start moving back toward the north."

"So every day the sun rises at a slightly different place than the day before." Now Mom looked at them solemnly. "Will the first rays of the sun rising on

Easter Sunday, March 22 strike the Chisos in the same place as the first rays of the sun rising on Easter Sunday, April 25?"

None of the upper graders would answer. Page kept silent because she knew now where this discussion was leading.

"No," said Belita at last. "You could not find anything that way."

"Are you saying there's no treasure?" Allis demanded.

"I'm not making a judgment on that," Mom said. "What I want you to see is how unfounded this story is if you apply what you've learned to it. My hope is that you'll never accept anything without first evaluating it in the light of what you know and what you can find out."

They went back to their desks with unhappy expressions to write the answer to the question. As they handed in their papers, it was as if they were giving up a dream they had long cherished.

"I can't get used to not believing that story," Allis said later. "Right now I wish I hadn't found out it isn't true." Page agreed, but with school closing for the Christmas holidays they soon recovered and began to talk of their discovery as an interesting job of detective work. Besides, Page and Allis agreed, only that particular story wasn't true. The treasure was still somewhere, waiting to be found.

17

THE WEEK BEFORE CHRISTMAS, Page and Mom went into town with the Lawrences to stay several days. Page had her janitor salary, counted and recounted, in an envelope, ready to buy gifts, and she hoped to start her horse book collection once again. As soon as they'd settled into the plain, old-time hotel, Page and Allis headed for Billy Newhouse's grocery store. What a lark to be in town, Page thought, as they skipped along on the sidewalks, and looked in shop windows. Christmas decorations, dancing and tinkling in the bracing wind, added to their excitement. Billy's store smelled like apples and oranges with the added earthy scent of nuts in the shell.

Cleofas, stacking boxes, smiled at them shyly. Billy kept busy with his accounts near the cash register, several customers crowding around him. Page and Allis looked all around for Carlotta. She wasn't there. They asked Cleofas. He pretended not to understand their English, though they used gestures, and Page even meowed.

Together they made a question in Spanish: *"Dónde el gato?"*

He continued to look blank.

"Carlotta!" Page shouted, trying to force him to understand.

He shrugged and went on with his work.

Something must have happened to Carlotta, Page thought. He won't tell us. She wheeled about and headed for Billy who was giving change to the last customer.

"Carlotta," she said breathlessly. "Where is she?"

A look passed between Billy and Cleofas. Then Billy made a little face and said, "That old cat! She might be somewhere in the back room." He stooped behind the counter, dismissing them.

They rushed to the storeroom, stacked high with groceries in reserve. It was not well lighted but before long in a back corner they found a large basket filled with soft old rags. In it, with half-closed eyes, lay Carlotta in all her white beauty. Nestled against her were three downy kittens with blue eyes barely opened.

The girls jumped up and down and shrieked in surprise and delight, causing Carlotta to start out of her drowsy state and frown her ears in displeasure. Immediately Page realized their error. She raised a finger to her lips to caution Allis. After that they softened their voices and slowed their movements. They stayed with Carlotta and the kittens a long while. They debated, in whispers, whether they dared hold the babies, but decided they had to wait for Carlotta's permission. When they left the storeroom, they promised her they'd be back. Out front, Billy Newhouse and Cleofas didn't try to hide their laughter.

"Surprised, weren't you?" Billy exulted. "Thought Carlotta had run off, didn't you?"

Cleofas said smoothly *"Dónde está la gata?"* correcting their Spanish.

Allis and Page laughed and hugged each other. Buttoning their jackets against the wind they hurried along the sidewalk to meet their mothers and tour the shops.

During their few days in town they visited the depot to say hello to Jame. "You're becoming a real Big Bender," he said to Page. "I can tell." She was surprised at how pleased she felt. They lunched at the cafe, where the cook's robust manners were not so frightening now, and the football player hobbled around on a crutch waiting tables.

Mr. Lawrence looked at him sympathetically. "Having a rough season, are you?"

"Yeah," he said. "We're busted up pretty bad, but the other teams are in worse shape."

Page wanted to see Domingo and Jack Spencer, but they were gone on the mail run, which was heavier than usual because of the Christmas season.

Late one afternoon with the skies darkening and snowflakes blowing, they met Clete on the street. He came with them to the old hotel for supper. Their table was drawn close to the great stone fireplace where a mesquite fire blazed. Page could feel the warmth from it, and the warmth of friendship in the laughter and talk that ebbed and flowed among them: Clete, Mr. and Mrs. Lawrence, Mom, Allis, Clay, and herself. She felt an easy happiness sitting there, not talking much, but listening, and not letting herself remember that the Lawrences would soon be leaving the Big Bend.

She and Allis told about Carlotta and her kittens. How everyone laughed when they repeated the Spanish question they had asked Cleofas. Clete told them *"los gatitos"* meant kittens, and taught them to say, *"Hay trés gatitos bonitos,"* which meant, "There are three pretty kittens." They planned to tell that to

Cleofas tomorrow when they made their return visit, and promised Clay he could come too.

When the supper party broke up, Clete told them he was returning to the border that night. He wished them a merry Christmas, and reached for his jacket on a wall peg. "I've something in my pockets for the treasure seekers," he said. He held out to Allis on the flat of his hand a tiny, perfect basket. Page recognized in an instant the woven pattern's similarity to the basket fragment in the lost cave. "A toy for a basket weaver's child," Clete explained. "When I was your age I found it in a cave not far from the Comanche trail."

Allis clasped it reverently. "This will be my Big Bend souvenir. I'll keep it always."

To Page he gave a chunk of clear green stone. As she held it close to the light, she saw gold gleaming in its heart.

"Ohhh, how beautiful," she said.

"From a mine in the State of Coahuila," he said.

Clay waited expectantly. Out of yet another pocket, Clete brought a satin-smooth, black-speckled rock the size of a potato. Allis's brother held it in his cupped hands.

"A dinosaur gizzard stone," Clete told him.

"Wow!" was all Clay could say.

The three of them stayed at the table examining their gifts while the grown-ups said their good-byes. As Clete went through the door, they suddenly remembered to call out their "thank yous" and their "Merry Christmases."

The next day, during their visit to Carlotta, Page, Allis, and Clay made Cleofas chuckle with their

Spanish sentence about the kittens. In the storeroom, they were careful to speak and move softly. Carlotta rewarded them by allowing each to hold a soft, mewing kitten. They smelled like warm milk. The girls claimed the two white ones because they were alike. Clay chose the spotted one for his own.

After more shopping and supper with Jame in the cafe, they set out for Panther Flat. The heavily ladened car hummed along through the Big Bend night, which was bright with moonlight on the white snow that still lingered. Page thought she'd never seen the landscape more beautiful. On the flat, the devil's witches lay quiet, but the jackrabbits danced madly, hundreds of them. It was such a wonder to see in the silver night the huge, long-eared rabbits leaping with their powerful hind legs and dancing in such a frenzy of joy that they woke Clay.

"They musta been eating loco weed," he decided, which made everybody laugh.

At the school, the Lawrences helped Page and Mom unload their packages. The two girls hugged each other, then turned to look long at the snow-dusted Chisos in the moonlight.

"I'll never, never forget the Big Bend," Allis said.

Her dad steered her toward the car where Clay had fallen asleep again. Page snuffled into her coat sleeve, watching them drive away.

"Oh, Mom, it was perfect! Thank you!"

Mom murmured agreement. They lugged everything inside and turned up the thermostat to warm their apartment. They didn't open anything or unpack their suitcases before collapsing bone tired into bed. But Page had the Mexico emerald with the heart of gold safe on the window ledge beside the Comanche chips. The last thing she saw before her eyes closed in sleep was the fern-green glow of the stone in a ray of moonlight.

18

PAGE HAD NOT SUCCEEDED in seeing a panther in the wild. However, one night returning late from the community center with the Lawrences, when they were the only car on the road, an unexplainable thing happened. In the area where everyone except Page could see Alsate, she noticed lights gleaming ahead of them. At first she thought it must be a highway post with reflectors, except no highway post would be on that side of the road. Neither would reflectors be so brilliant, so alive.

Mrs. Lawrence leaned forward, peering through the windshield. "Whatever in the world is that?"

With everyone watching, the lights vanished and a long shadow crossed the road in an extraordinary way. Page could not describe the movement. She only knew that it was different from anything she'd ever seen before.

Mr. Lawrence zoomed ahead to the spot, and whirled the car crosswise on the road so the headlights shone in the direction the shadow went. Nothing. They waited without talking for a long time, then Mr. Lawrence exhaled as if he'd been holding his breath and said, "I wonder what THAT was."

They all guessed, "Panther!" except Page who said with a tinge of jealousy, "The spirit of Alsate!" She felt left out because she was the only one who could never see Alsate, so she meant this as sort of a joke, but Allis took her seriously.

"Oh, no," she said. "It was more like a panther."

"But we've seen panthers often at night, and none of them ever looked like that," Mrs. Lawrence insisted.

Allis's dad kept a thoughtful silence the rest of the way home. When he stopped the car at the school, before Page and Mom made a move to get out, he said, "There've been several reports of a black panther in the park, all of them so vague I've discounted them. What we saw tonight almost makes me a believer." He gave a little laugh. "It's possible that one came down out of the mountains of Mexico and crossed the Rio Grande. Panthers travel far."

The excitement of a black panther roaming the park kept Page awake that night. She sat for a long while at the window that overlooked the water pan, wondering and hoping that it might come to drink.

But in the days that followed, due mostly to the Lawrences' preparations for moving, the puma slipped to the back of her thoughts. She and Mom attended several farewell parties, down on the river, up in the mountains, and at ranches outside the park boundaries. Page had fun at all of them because she didn't yet believe that Allis, her first and only best friend, was truly leaving.

Not until the very night before the moving van was to come, when a small group gathered in the walled garden at the Allman house for supper, did she face what all the fun parties meant. Now she knew that saying good-bye was a reality.

Mr. Allman, as night came on, lit a bonfire of fragrant mesquite wood. All of them—Mr. and Mrs. Allman and Doug, Mr. and Mrs. Lawrence and Clay and Allis, Clete, Page and Mom—drew their chairs close, talked about the years the Lawrences had spent in the Big Bend, and about what their future in Maine might hold for them. Page had little to say, looking and listening. Many thoughts flitted through her mind, most of them having nothing to do with the Lawrences leaving. Within these head-high walls Doug had kept Victorio just before he was killed; outside the walls, only a couple of houses away, lived Hank Boatwright, who'd never been punished for what he and Mack Hill did to Victorio. She watched Clete across the leaping flames, dressed in white, his dark Comanche looks accentuated by the shadows, looks that had made her distrust him until she learned what a generous and kind person he was.

She was remembering the canyon rescue when out of the corner of her eye she saw a piece of the dark night drop soundlessly on top of the rock wall. In one sinuous movement the darkness stretched itself out, and lay there perfectly still, its shining yellow eyes watching them with intent curiosity. The black panther! No one made a sudden move, no one raised a voice, but an electric charge shot through the group, and Page knew everyone was aware of the spectator. She thought she would suffocate from her thudding heart which seemed to swell till it filled her chest. Each person acted naturally, but each contrived to

take a look before the big cat rose, gathered itself together, and, without a sound, leaped back the way it

had come. The long, elegant tail was the last thing Page saw disappear.

The girls jumped up and hugged each other, laughing with excitement.

"Alsate's farewell gift to you," Clete suggested with a smile.

"I know!" Allis said, grinning, as if she had expected it.

The next day Page watched from the patio as the huge moving van pulled out of the Lawrence drive. Then the family followed it in their familiar car, Allis waving out the back window and Page waving from the school until they disappeared in the far distance.

Page cried some and gave way to a lonely and aimless feeling. Sometimes she walked past the empty Lawrence house, hoping that Allis would open the door and call an excited greeting. During the difficult days that followed, Page did a reckless thing, something that she knew she shouldn't do without first talking to Mom.

Studying the calendar, counting the days since Allis left, and looking ahead to when the Lawrences should reach their new home, she realized that Dad's birthday was coming soon. She decided to make a card for him, a pretty one with a happy birthday message inside. She'd have to work on it in secret, and sneak to the mailbox with it. She convinced herself this was an okay thing to do because she would just sign her name, not give an address or anything else that could be traced. She well remembered how Mom's friend Lorna had stressed they must not contact Dad in any way for their own safety. In the Big Bend, the few letters Mom received from Lorna had repeated those warnings. But the passing of time had dimmed Page's remembrance of the bad things that happened back home, as if she had imagined them. She hummed while creating the card for Dad, anticipating how surprised he'd be when he found it in his mailbox. She signed it, "I love you, Page Williams."

With her best friend gone for good, Page took more notice of her other classmates. One day she came in from play period to find Epifanio frowning over a lesson. "What's the matter?" she asked.

"This—this English makes no sense," he said, shaking his head. "Spanish language is easy. You can understand it."

Page was ready to deny that, but after all, she'd spoken only English all her life, and Epifanio spoke Spanish and English. Surely he'd know better than she did. "How do you mean?"

"Well, look," he said desperately. "What's your name?"

"Page," she said hesitantly.

"You spell it how?"

She told him, wondering what he was trying to say.

"And what's this?" He flipped open the book he held.

"A leaf. A page. Ohhh, I see."

"*Sí.* A leaf grows on trees. A page is in a book, but it is also you." He wagged his head. "And the name of Allis's brother is Clay. But clay comes out of the earth—it is dirt. I don't understand English."

After that she tried to be more aware when others struggled with problems. For one thing, she saw that arithmetic always stymied Margaret. It wasn't an easy subject for Page either, but working together, they found they could get results. Page began to see some of the reasons Mom became a teacher. To help someone to an understanding was kind of like a miracle.

A surprising thing that developed out of the arithmetic lessons was a friendship with Margaret. Not an everyday friendship but a spend-the-day-and-night friendship. It really began when Mom had to go away for a teachers' meeting. School closed for two days. With the Lawrences no longer in Panther Flat, Mom didn't want to leave Page at the apartment by herself.

"Why, send her down to the river with us," Gypsy Meg boomed.

19

WHAT AN EXCITEMENT! The river was another world, as Page well knew from what she saw of it on barbecue day. So after school on Wednesday, Page loaded her suitcase in the back of Gypsy Meg's pickup, and away they went winding down the narrow river road.

Margaret's pale cheeks flushed with excitement too. "What a good time we'll have! You can become friends with Carmencita."

The long adobe house looked different without the crowds of people. It was so quiet that Page could hear the singsong of the river from the shady porch. They left her suitcase in the room she was to share with Margaret, a room that opened onto the veranda. Then they went to find the greatest wonder, Carmencita, who was taking her *siesta* on the living-room rug. She bounded up to meet Gypsy Meg, standing on her hind legs, front paws on Gypsy Meg's shoulders, sniffing her face, kissing her.

Gypsy Meg embraced the big cat, whispering in her dark furred ear, *"Hola!* My Mexican tiger! Catamount! Lion of God!"

Carmencita dropped to all fours, twining round

and round Gypsy Meg's legs, purring loud as a motor without a muffler. Page sank to the floor in amazement, watching the panther's powerful muscles bulging in her legs and rippling along her body under her golden coat. She wanted to pet Carmencita right away, but Gypsy Meg said Page must wait until the puma offered to be friends.

"Carmencita makes the first move," Margaret's grandma said. "Be patient."

Page sighed. "It's hard to be patient."

Gypsy Meg laughed. "But it's a good trait to possess, and not only when you're befriending *leones.*"

They stayed with Carmencita, talking to her and about her, letting her become familiar with Page. "You should have seen how tiny she was, and half-starved when she was brought here," Gypsy Meg said.

"And sick, too," Margaret said. "Grandma slept with her to keep her warm and fed her with a baby bottle every two hours—all night and all day."

"No wonder Carmencita loves her so much," Page said, moving to sit near, but not touching, the big cat. Carmencita now lay in a patch of sunlight, regarding them with her greenish-gold eyes set at a slant in her broad face. "She is so beautiful! I can't believe it!"

Carmencita curved one of her large forepaws and began licking and gnawing at the claws, just as Page had seen Carlotta do. Gypsy Meg in the meantime left the room. Page didn't miss her until suddenly Carmencita sat up and whistled, loud and clear, like a person.

Margaret nudged Page with delight. "Watch her! Listen!" Carmencita went to the different doors leading out of the room, whistling and searching. From far off they heard Gypsy Meg call the panther's name, and Carmencita, with a lash of her tail, bounded out of sight.

Margaret laughed. "She always does that. Whenever Grandma's out of sight, she whistles."

"You let her free outside?"

"Yes, but we stay with her. Everybody knows Carmencita, but we don't want anybody to hurt her," Margaret explained, "or her to hurt anybody. She hates little kids."

The girls went outside to visit Margaret's favorite places. They explored abandoned houses built of the pinkish-beige river rocks that were put together, tight and neat, without mortar to mar them. They walked over low rounded hills covered with dead ferns.

"Why did all these ferns die?" Page asked.

"They're not dead," Margaret assured her. "They're resurrection plants. When rain comes, this hill will turn green again."

"That can't be true." Page knelt to examine the dry brown leaves curling in on themselves. "They're dead!"

Margaret uprooted a plant. "Keep this one as long as you want. When you're ready for it to come alive put it in water. You'll see."

Page tucked it in her pocket.

"Now to the hot baths!" Margaret skipped away downriver. "Tomorrow we can get in the tub."

At river's edge a clear hot spring gushed out of the ground, flowing into a coffin-like box hewn into the rock. "We bathe here every day. Grandma says it'll make me strong and healthy," Margaret smiled wistfully. "She makes me drink the water too." Her face twisted, and she gagged with her tongue hanging out. "Tastes like sulfur and a lot of other stuff."

"I won't drink a drop of river water." Page shuddered. "Jack Spencer says it casts a spell on you so that you'll never leave the Big Bend."

"I never want to leave," Margaret said. "Where would there be a better place?" She looked from horizon to horizon, her face shining.

At a shallow place, they removed their shoes and waded across to Mexico. They followed the river toward the west along a path worn down ankle deep.

"The old Comanche trail," Margaret said. "From long, long ago, but Mexicans still use it."

They went to the ruins of the Spanish mission and stood in the doorway, gazing toward the Chisos. Being there was like living a dream, Page thought. She couldn't shake the magical feeling even after Margaret said, "It's sunset now instead of sunrise, but anybody with good sense can see your mom was right about that treasure legend."

Page laughed. "I don't mind now, but I did at first."

They made the return trip in the deepening twilight, waded the river to reclaim their shoes, and started toward home. Coming to meet them was another part of the dream, Gypsy Meg in her flowing costume accompanied by Carmencita. The panther seemed to take pleasure in smelling odors along the way, especially blossoms. A faraway look came over her face, and her eyes half shut. Talking in murmurs as if fearful of disturbing Carmencita and the coming night, they returned to the river house together under the watchful Big Bend stars.

During her four-day visit, Page's delight was the panther. As soon as Carmencita allowed her, Page pressed face-to-face with her, mingling their breathing, and murmuring to her. It was a painful reminder of Victorio, but she did it as a step toward winning the friendship of Carmencita. The markings of the panther's face fascinated Page, especially the white fur patches on either side of her pink-tipped nose.

"This is her butterfly," Margaret said, tracing the black hairs that outlined it.

The big cat seemed to accept their adoration with a gleam of humor in her gold-green eyes, which Page decided were the most beautiful part of this incredibly beautiful animal.

"I'm trying to remember some words in my book back home," Page said, gazing into Carmencita's eyes. "It's about cats' eyes shining—cha—chatoyant. *Chatoyant lustre!* That's it! I love those words. They're French."

"Now you gave them to me, and I love them too. The *chatoyant lustre* of Carmencita's eyes *es muy bonita,*" Margaret crooned as the three of them lay in the sun on the living-room floor. "Carmencita *es muy bonita.*"

"*Muy, muy, muy bonita,*" Page agreed lazily.

Carmencita went with them to their daily hot bath. She had no interest in the hot springs, but with absolute grace took a swim in the river, then came out to drowse on a flat rock until the girls finished.

Jack Spencer and Domingo came late Sunday afternoon for a brief visit, but he said the girls had to play
with Domingo in the mail van.

"I don't trust Carmencita," Mr. Spencer said.
"Panthers like tender little dogs for dessert."

"Not Carmencita!" Page and Margaret both exclaimed, but they knew better than to risk it.

With the resurrection plant in her suitcase, Page
went back to the schoolhouse in the mail van.
Domingo snuffled all over her, wagging his tail and
growling. "That's Carmencita odor!" Page explained.

Mom was home from her meeting, and had supper
ready. "How was the river?" she asked, her eyes
sparkling.

"It was wonderful—so wonderful I can't talk about
it—at least not yet. Mom, is Margaret sick?"

Mom kept silent. Page knew she couldn't reveal
anything from school records, but Page felt anxious
about her friend.

"Rheumatic fever," Jack Spencer offered. "Pretty serious, but her grandmother takes good care of her."

"Oh, oh!" Page said distressed.

"If anybody can help her, it's Gypsy Meg," Jack Spencer reassured her.

One of the first things Page did was prepare a pot and set out the resurrection plant. She kept it well watered, and almost immediately tiny speckles of green began showing. Page was the only one in school who thought that was remarkable; the others were too accustomed to the miracle.

20

WITH THE END OF SCHOOL fast approaching, the
school board was forced to call another meeting
of the parents to discuss with Mom how she was running the school. The changes she had made did not
satisfy the most vocal ones—the Hills, the Boatwrights,
and probably the Powells, Page thought. The board
suggested that if the parents had a frank discussion
with Mom perhaps some of the misunderstandings
could be cleared up.

Mom held little hope for that. "Looks as if they'll
be satisfied only when I'm fired," she said.

Mr. Allman, as board president, presided over the
meeting. Bret and Bart sat with their parents near the
front. Tonight was the first time the Powells had ever
been to the school. Page smiled to see how much the
twins looked like their dad, freckles, red hair, and
all. She listened from the back row as the Hills and
Boatwrights made their accusations one by one. When
they finally paused, several other parents expressed
support of Mom's teaching. Gypsy Meg, for one, said
Margaret was learning more than she had at any other
school, and enjoying it. "Schooling's not supposed to

be dull, or painful," she continued. "Learning should be a privilege and a joy."

"That's another thing," Mrs. Hill interrupted, tossing her blond head. "How can anybody who's never been to school judge what a school should be?" Her pretty face distorted into a sneer. "And when the teacher allows her daughter to associate with a—a river renegade, a gypsy fortune teller, what can we expect for the school—"

Astonished exclamations drowned out her voice. Mr. Allman demanded order. In a calm voice he said, "This discussion will be kept to an impersonal level. Mrs. Hill, will you retract that statement?"

"You'll get no retraction from me. I meant every word of it."

Mr. Powell then stood up and cleared his throat. Mr. Allman nodded permission for him to speak. Page tensed, wondering what he would say. Bret and Bart, beside him, kept still.

"My wife and I have reserved judgment on the teacher," he said. "Perhaps for too long. But we want it known now that our boys are having an outstanding school year. They've not only learned a great deal, but learning has been an excitement for them. Whatever way the teacher is running the school, it's good for Bret and Bart, and we're behind her one hundred percent."

Mom's face sort of fell apart because this tribute was so unexpected. But then Mrs. Boatwright put in about how the whole school was idling on the playground that day, "looking at a cloud," when they should have been inside studying. "I would never have wasted time that way when I was teaching," she said.

Mrs. Hill added, "And they write stories and draw pictures when they should be doing spelling and arithmetic and reading. They play act about planets and the moon. Imagine! They'll never learn anything!"

Clete spoke for the absent ranch family, saying that he knew how well pleased they were with the progress made by Sam, Lily, and Travis. He turned to Mom. "Travis could not read when he started school. Isn't he reading on sixth grade level now?" Mom nodded. Clete looked at the Hills and the Boatwrights. "It may be that you are expecting a perfect teacher," he said. "But Mrs. Williams isn't perfect. She is human, just as the rest of us are. It isn't easy for her to meet the needs of so many children who are so different from each other. Teaching every subject to seven grades within about six hours is also difficult. From my point of view as a board member, she is doing an excellent job."

What an astonishing long speech from Clete! Mrs. Blackwell, the mother of Kathy and Mary, who had replaced Mrs. Lawrence on the board, agreed with Clete. After more discussion, Mom in a steady voice pointed out how she had adapted her teaching methods lately in an effort to please the disgruntled parents. "But that's as far as I can go," she said. "Learning should be an adventure, a discovery, and I must have the freedom to teach that way. I am sorry if some of you are displeased. I will continue to do the best I can until the end of the school year. Then if you feel I've failed, you can refuse to renew my contract for next year."

"Why not give all the students a standardized test?" Mrs. Hill suggested. "That would show whether or not they're learning what they should."

Mrs. Boatwright nodded agreement.

"You realize," Mom said, "a test would measure not only what students have learned this year, but what they've learned in previous years. Unless they've had good teaching before I came, this partial year could not catch them up to all they should know now."

Mrs. Boatwright's eyes widened. After a short silence she said with a shrug, "It's just a suggestion."

"Something to consider," Mrs. Hill added. "Maybe later."

The meeting ended soon after that. Page wondered whether their lives might be free of strain now. At least the Powells had declared themselves, and Bret and Bart looked happy about that.

A second surprise that came out of the meeting was Mrs. Hill calling Gypsy Meg a "river renegade," "a gypsy fortune teller." How did Mack's mother know Page had spent that long weekend with Margaret? More work of the Chisos spirits? Sometimes there did seem to be something supernatural about how rumors and gossip spread over far distances in the Big Bend.

Page remembered with pleasure her visit to the river. To make herself smile, or feel happy, all she had to do was think over those four riverside days. She longed to be invited again. Never in her life had she known a renegade, but if Gypsy Meg was one, she'd like to meet others.

One Saturday when Clete came to take them to the rodeo in town, Page had a few minutes with him on the porch while waiting for Mom. She knew him well enough now to be sure he would level with her. "Why did Mrs. Hill call Gypsy Meg a renegade?" she asked.

"She is in a way, don't you think?" He smiled at her.

Page drew pictures in the dust with the toe of her boot—she was proud of the cowboy boots she now owned—while Clete leaned against a post. "Well, she's different. But renegade's bad, isn't it?"

Clete grew serious. "For one thing, it has to do with the panther. Some people think she should not have it."

"But she saved Carmencita's life!" Page protested.

"Yes. But people disregard that. More important though, the park has been pressuring Meg for a long time to release Carmencita. 'No wild animals in captivity' is an unbendable rule."

"Carmencita couldn't live in the wild. Somebody would kill her right away. She wouldn't even know to be afraid." Page's voice rose in indignation.

"Of even more importance is the panther's danger to humans."

"Ohh, yes. She hates little kids!" Page had forgotten that. "What a nightmare if she were turned loose!"

Mom came out then, looking very unteacherly in her Western garb, and they took off in the white pickup for town and the rodeo, following in the dust of everybody else from the Big Bend.

21

THE RODEO REMINDED PAGE OF A CIRCUS in many ways—people eating popcorn and hot dogs and drinking soda pop. Friends from far-spread ranches greeted each other joyfully, and kids ran around in the dust and sun. From their seats with Margaret and Gypsy Meg, they saw the Allmans in front, the Hills and the Boatwrights off to the side.

"Hank performs after the barrel races," Margaret pointed to the program. It said "Champion bullwhip master, Hank Boatwright".

"I don't know what that means," Page said, uninterested.

"I don't like it," Margaret said. "Too loud, too scary."

The girls admired the horses, and cheered for the calves that had to endure roping. When Hank's turn came, Page was instantly alert when he walked into the ring, dressed in black, carrying a long slim black thing in his hand. She stared, struggling with a memory. Not until the whip began to crack—sharp, piercing, like a mountain splitting open or a lightning flash—did Page realize what was happening. She sat frozen in the hot sun, her heart threatening to burst from her chest. The crowd clapped and cheered each skilled trick with the long black writhing whip. A perspiring, red-faced man roared, "Make that black snake sing, boy!"

At an intense high point—crack after crack of the whip—Mack Hill leaped up in the grandstand and gave a carrying cry, joined by Hank in the ring. It was the savage war cry of Apaches and Comanches going into battle to destroy each other. Page covered her ears against the sound and sobbed, "No! Don't!" If only

she could have been there at the corral that night to stop them! To save Victorio!

Mom pulled her back to the seat, searching her face with concern. "What is it?"

Page hid her face against Mom's shoulder, pressing her hands tighter over her ears, but she could still hear.

After a while Mom relaxed her hold. "Now it's over," she said, keeping her arm around Page and offering her a handkerchief. Page wiped her tears, waiting for her body to stop trembling. She knew what she had to do.

Intermission came. Page took her time weaving through the crowd to where the Allmans stood talking to friends. This might not be the right time or place, but Page knew she couldn't hold silent any longer. She tugged Mr. Allman's sleeve, and asked if she could speak to him. No one noticed as they stood to one side, the noise of the crowd swirling around them.

"You said if I remembered anything—if I thought of something—about—about Victorio, to tell you." Her words stumbled out, though she tried to steady her voice.

He nodded.

"Well, what I heard that night—it was Hank Boatwright's bull whip. And the yell was like that one he gave at the end, with Mack Hill."

Mr. Allman raised his head, searching the crowd, looking toward the boys. "Are you sure? Is there any way you could be mistaken?"

"No way. I'm absolutely sure." She told him the part she'd left out before and a great relief flooded through her. She didn't care what happened now.

After that last meeting with the parents, she realized that Mom could cope with whatever came. I will too, she thought. I'm finished with hiding things.

Mr. Allman touched her shoulder. "Thank you, Page. We'll talk more later. Now, go enjoy!"

Doug was watching as she left his dad. Page gave a little wave and said, "See you later." She would wait until Mr. Allman took action before telling Doug the story. Would it be easier for him, knowing what had happened that night—or harder? No matter. It was his right to know.

Later Page could recall few details of her first rodeo. The unexpected solution to the mystery that had worried her for such a long time overshadowed all else. Recovering from her first fright, she awaited the confrontation calmly. She talked with Mom about it when Mr. Allman called an after-school meeting of the Boatwrights, the Hills, and Page in his office at park headquarters.

"Want me to go with you?" Mom asked.

Page decided not. She had the feeling that Mr. Allman believed she could handle it alone, or he would have asked Mom to come. Leaving Mom out of it was a way of distancing her from the problem, too, though the boys' families might not see it that way.

The Boatwrights and Hills came in their cars and picked up the two boys to attend the meeting. Page walked, which made her the last to arrive. The office seemed crowded and too warm with all of them sitting around Mr. Allman's desk. Mack and Hank looked sullen. Page clasped her hands in her lap, forcing herself to sit still and to breathe deeply.

"I don't understand what this is all about," Mrs. Hill said.

"I regret to have to ask you to come here." Mr. Allman eyes went slowly round the group, lingering on the boys. "You remember what happened the night of the welcome party for the teacher." It was a statement, not a question.

"We weren't there," Mrs. Boatwright protested. "Of course we don't remember."

"Hank and Mack were there," Mr. Allman stated.

The boys contorted their faces in denials, but he shushed them.

"Page, please tell us where you were that night." Mr. Allman, looking at the others, added sternly, "No interruptions."

Page faced Doug's dad and made herself speak in a steady voice as if the two of them were alone. She told how the two boys watched the party through the window, how the taller boy said, "Let's do it now," and how they disappeared. Then came the noise of the cracking whip and the maniacal shriek, the same sounds she had heard at the rodeo.

"That doesn't prove anything," Hank Boatwright said. "Just because SHE says so."

"I saw the whip in your hand," Page said. "I heard what you said. I heard what happened."

The boys and their parents steadfastly denied any knowledge of that night, though Mr. Allman and Page just as steadfastly accused them.

In the end, Mr. Allman said, "We all know who was responsible for what happened. We all know that lives were endangered, that property was damaged." He looked down at his desk. "We know that a fine horse died, a horse that was loved by my son. Doug will someday get over what happened, but he will never forget it. I won't forget it either. As long as you boys live in this park, as long as you go to school here, you can be sure I'm watching." Page could not believe that brown eyes could look so hard as Mr. Allman's, sweeping the half circle of set faces around his desk. "From now on, you're both on probation. One wrong move and that's it." He stood up, abruptly dismissing them. "Page, will you stay a moment?" After the door closed, he said, "What about Doug? Are you going to tell him?"

"I thought he ought to know," she said.

"After all these months, to tell him will open wounds that are healing. It will make him hate these two boys. Now he doesn't hate anyone. I'd like to keep it that way." He stood silent, his hand on the door. "However, I trust your judgment as his friend. Whatever you decide is all right with me."

"Will you talk to him about it? Or is it just between him and me?"

"If he asks me, I'll talk to him about it. But knowing Doug, he'll not ask." He sighed. "Doug doesn't say much, but he feels deep. That can be hard on a fellow."

"Yes, I know," Page said. "I'll think about it."

"Thanks for coming," he said, smiling. "And thanks for being such an asset to the teacher. We're lucky to have you."

Page was thrilled speechless. She could only smile back at him and head for the path down in the arroyo and up to the schoolhouse.

In her thoughts she argued back and forth whether or not to tell Doug. It was like wrestling with a devil's witch. She finally decided to ask him to come for a hike, and see how things developed. Hurrying past Allis's still-empty house, she noticed a red and yellow kite rise in the wind above Doug's yard.

"Let's go fly it from Lone Mountain," she shouted over the Allmans' rock wall.

"Sure." Doug wound the kite down out of the limitless blue, and tucking it under his arm they headed for the nearby mountain. They easily got the kite airborne and sat on boulders watching it skip about in the changeable wind. Page loved the view from the top of Lone Mountain—miles and miles across the flat toward the mountain ranges that stood between them and town. The few cars coming and going looked like bugs. As she and Doug talked lazily in the warm sun, they watched one of the cars come into Panther Flat, then branch off onto the schoolhouse road.

"Somebody who's lost." Page dismissed it lightly. She gloried in the sun-warmed wind with the cool under bite. "I wish I could flap my arms and fly away, and away." She stood up waving her arms, the wind belling out her jacket.

Doug let the kite have a loose rein. They stayed for an hour, taking turns flying the kite. Once while she had control and Doug lay on his back on a boulder, his face covered by his cap, she said, "You know Victorio? I think of him a lot. I sure wanted to ride him. I hoped that I'd have a chance."

"Yeah," said Doug from under his cap. "Yeah. I rode him, lots of times. Sometimes I dream about him. He's in horse heaven, I know—no panthers, no loco weed, lots of water and juicy grass. He's got friends there too, other horses."

"He's happy then," said Page winding in the kite.

"Yeah. He's plenty happy." When he removed the cap from his face and sat up, his eyes shone unnaturally bright. "He was named for an Apache chief."

"I know," Page said. "I saw his picture in the legend book."

"This summer my dad's getting me another horse. We'll board him at a ranch outside the park. Want me to teach you to ride?"

"Sure," was the only answer she could manage, dizzy as she was with unexpected joy.

The kite, on a short length of string, turned rebellious and refused to be caught. As Page tried to reel it in, Doug chased and leaped after it. It eluded him every time, almost as if playing a game. Their time on the mountain ended in a long, foolish laughing spell, and Page came down to the flat satisfied that not telling Doug was the right decision for now. She felt in a way that she had left her hatred of Hank and Mack on the mountaintop, washed clean by the wild wind and purified by the sun.

22

PAGE HAD FORGOTTEN THE STRANGE CAR they had watched from the top of Lone Mountain. She was surprised to find it parked on the playground. As she walked closer, she saw, with a shock of recognition, the dusty Alabama license plate. Dad's car! How had he found them? The birthday card? But she hadn't given a clue, she was sure. She trembled with panic and happiness. She wanted to jerk the door open, yet she feared what she'd find. Oh, Mom! Don't, please don't be mad! Oh, Dad, please, please behave!

She pushed into the school. The apartment door stood open. Dad sat in the big chair, tan and relaxed. She couldn't see Mom, but she heard her saying, "You shouldn't have come. You had no right to come."

Dad jumped to his feet when he saw Page and came toward her smiling. "Page! Thanks for your birthday card. Do you know, it was the only greeting I got."

"Hello, Dad." Shyness made the words almost inaudible.

Mom stood with her back against the stove, her face white, her eyes accusing.

Page felt sad that she had betrayed her, but she

hadn't meant to. "How did you find us? I didn't put a return address on the card."

His smile widened. "The postmark. It said Big Bend National Park, Texas. I'd never heard of the place, but I found out about it quick enough. Now I've come to take you home—both of you."

"It's not that simple," Mom said, her voice tight. "I have obligations here. I've signed a contract till the end of the school year. And I have to know that our lives will be different from before."

"Things will be different. I promise. And you should see how I've fixed up the house. You'll like the kitchen—new cupboards, indirect lighting—and bigger bookcases in the living room. I made them myself. You saw my new car. It's a little dusty now. These roads are awful."

"Those aren't the important things. Are you getting help? Are you in treatment so you can behave differently? That's what matters."

"You've sure grown," Dad continued, smiling at Page. "You'll soon be old enough to drive my new car. Come outside and I'll show it to you. Maybe you'd like to drive it around out back?"

"Answer me!" Mom said. "Are you in counseling so we can have a decent life together? Are you taking the medication the doctor prescribed?"

Dad gave a little apologetic shake of his head. "Not yet, Ellie. I've not had time, but I will. I promise, if you come home, I'll do all that."

"Promises! You've made lots of promises, and they've always been worthless. Once you get us back there, things might go well for awhile, then it'll be like before. And I can't live like that. I won't live like that anymore. You've hit me for the last time—"

Dad glanced at Page. "Maybe she ought to go outside. She shouldn't hear—"

"I'm sorry she has to hear it, but she knows. She saw what went on. Since you're here, and since this affects her too, she should stay and have input."

"I can't believe how different you are. Where's my sweet Ellie?"

"Your sweet Ellie is gone. I've outgrown her. This Ellie stands on her own feet. She has a say-so in what happens in her life. She is a person, and she's going to be treated like a person—no beatings, no black eyes, no broken eyeglasses." Her voice thinned to a whisper. "No butcher knives, no guns—none of that has a place in this Ellie's life."

Page hurt to hear Mom say those words. She hurt to remember that those terrible times had really happened. She knew that she could not go back to enduring fear, every day being pulled apart by two people she loved. She would not have Mom go back to such a life either, even to keep their family together.

Dad sat in the chair as if he were established permanently, arguing sometimes, pleading other times. He blamed Mom for "running off" and "kidnapping his only child." Tears rolled down his cheeks and dripped on his shirt. He kept on talking without wiping them. "I can't tell you how many sleepless nights I've had, worrying whether you were safe, if somebody had hurt you. Page, if anybody ever hurt you or did you wrong, I'd make him suffer for it the rest of his life. That's how much I love you. That's what I'd do for you." He talked on and on, blaming himself for not making more money so Mom would be happier, blaming his parents for how they raised him.

Page had heard it all before, but never in such detail and at such length. She was numb with weariness. Her eyes drooped. She wanted to yawn but didn't dare.

Mom said, "You must leave. Page and I have to get up for school tomorrow. It's the last day—I have to see to all kinds of things—the closing program—"

Dad interrupted, "But it's my life you're throwing away. Without you and Page, what do I have to live for? I might as well kill myself and be finished. You're thinking only of yourself."

Back home, these threats had terrified Page. Dad brought up suicide when all his other arguments failed. He knew that was a sure way to make Mom give in to him. Page had also thought then that maybe Mom was selfish to do something she wanted to do like getting a college degree, but now she could clearly see that Dad was the one thinking of himself and what he wanted. And the main thing he wanted was to have them in his power again. He didn't care that Mom had a hard day tomorrow and that the clock hands pointed to midnight.

Page stood up, rubbing her eyes. "I'm too tired. I have to go to bed."

Dad grabbed her hand. "Page, Page! You'll come back with me, I know you will. Your card said 'I love you.' I memorized that—it's kept me going." He clung so hard to her hand she almost cried out, but she didn't dare shake off his grip.

"Dad, I have to go to bed. I'm dizzy. I can't think. . . ."

"You go on to bed. Your mom and I can settle this without you."

"But this is where I sleep," she said, untying her shoes.

"Oh, well. Come outside, Ellie. You've got to see that I'm right. Your place is at home, with me. You know you promised 'till death do us part.'"

"You made promises too," Mom said. "But this can't go on. You have to leave." She made as if to usher him out, but suddenly stepped backward when she saw the expression on his face.

Turning to Page she said, "Go on to bed. I'll be outside just for a little while."

"No, Mom. Don't go!" Page remembered that look. It had always signaled an end to his talking and a beginning of his beatings.

Mom calmly locked the front door. "Make the bed," she said. "Get your pajamas on." She followed Dad out through the school, leaving the apartment door open.

Page trembled so violently she could hardly unfold the sofa or spread the blanket. Through her tears she groped for the pillows in the closet. But she would not undress. She put on her shoes, and got the flashlight ready. If she heard Dad mistreating Mom, she'd leave by the patio door and race through the rocks and thorns of the arroyo to rouse Mr. Allman. She was finished with keeping Dad's secret. As she stood poised, listening, Mom ran in from the playground, slamming shut the door from the apartment to the school.

"Quick! Turn out the light!" Page heard the door lock click into place.

Together in the darkness they shoved the chest of drawers against the door. On the other side, Dad cursed and yelled, falling over desks, searching for the light switch. Page knew when he found it. The light, springing on, outlined the door. She and Mom stood like sticks watching the dark door. Dad jerked the knob. It held firm. Cursing, he began ramrodding the door with his shoulder.

"Open this door," he yelled. "Don't you dare lock me out!"

Mom and Page backed against the chest, holding it tight to the door. Now he was pounding the door with many different things, like a bombardment. Glass shattered.

"Open the door, or I'll trash this place." A loud crash sounded like a bookcase overturning. The door trembled under a barrage of heavy boot kicks. "Open up!"

Suddenly, there was quiet in the schoolroom.

"Who are you?" Dad demanded furiously.

"What's the problem here?" Mr. Allman's voice sounded calm, almost friendly.

Dad hesitated, then he managed to sputter, "She won't let me in." Metal clanked as he picked up pieces of something. "Sorry I broke this."

"Don't worry about it." Mr. Allman was nearer now. "Take a breather. Come outside and talk things over."

"I didn't mean for this to happen," Dad said, his voice moving away from them. "It's her fault. She wouldn't let me in."

"I know," Mr. Allman said. "Maybe we can work something out."

The door to the playground opened and shut.

Mom and Page stood tense in the dark, their arms around each other, listening. In the silence, Page could hear her own ragged breathing, as if she couldn't get enough air. She marveled that Mr. Allman knew how to disarm Dad with a calm friendly approach. What would happen now? Would Dad convince him that nothing was wrong?

In the quiet night, two motors started up and drove away. Someone came in the back door. Page thought she would faint not knowing who was there. Had she and Mom been left alone with Dad?

"Mrs. Williams," Mr. Allman called. "Page! It's all right now. Open the door."

They turned on the light, shoved the chest of drawers aside, and stepped out into the wreckage of the school.

"Are you unhurt?" he asked.

"Yes," said Mom in a shaky voice. "But you came just in time. How did you know?"

Page picked up the broken pot with the resurrection plant in it.

"We were aware that a man in the campground was making persistent inquiries about you. When Clete drove past just now on the river road, he was concerned to see the schoolhouse lights on at midnight. He came by my house. I was up by then—the noise awakened me."

Dad had kicked out the window glass by Mom's desk, torn up her final reports that were ready to present to the board, and scattered the pieces across the floor. Books were flung everywhere, and the globe with its axis broken lay in a corner. Overturned desks spilled out their contents, and the library table was tilted on its side.

"What'll happen now? Are we safe?" Mom asked through pale lips.

Page began gathering and stacking books.

"Leave that," Mr. Allman said. "Go to bed now. You're safe. Clete is escorting him out of the park, and sending him on his way. As long as you are here, he cannot come back. I will alert all the rangers to watch for him. He cannot return to this park." Page found it reassuring to hear Mr. Allman say the same thing over and over: Dad could not come back to the Big Bend. She and Mom would be safe.

"I can't let the students find their school like this," Mom said. "Nothing must be allowed to spoil tomorrow."

"Everything will go well tomorrow--that is, today," Mr. Allman said. "But the teacher must get some rest so she'll be in good shape." He smiled faintly. "I'll have a crew over here early to take care of this. Good night, now." Mom began to protest, but he gently guided them into the apartment and closed the door behind them.

Page's body ached as she stretched out in bed. In the dark, she did two things she hadn't done since she was small—she kissed her mother good night and said her prayers.

Early next morning she awakened to muffled sounds in the schoolroom. She sat up, clutching the blanket to her in fright, until she remembered Mr. Allman's promise to "have a crew over" to straighten things up. She didn't see how anybody could bring order out of the chaos Dad had created. Mom still slept soundly. Page sighed and snuggled down for more sleep.

The last day of school was a great day, as Mr. Allman predicted. Page was amazed at the transformation the crew had brought about. They'd moved some bookcases in front of the broken windows and swept up the glass. They'd replaced the books on the shelves, straightened the kids' desks, and mended the globe. Only someone who was particularly looking for evidence of wreckage could have found any. Anyway, the kids were all too excited to notice. They spent the morning setting up the program they planned to present for their parents in the afternoon.

Mom looked pale, with dark circles under her eyes, but she was rested and calm. The torn pieces of her final reports for the school board were piled on her desk. She took them into the apartment, to piece together and recopy. Fortunately, the students' report cards had been kept safe in a locked drawer of her desk.

Last night Page would not have believed that today could be so bright in every way. For the parents, the kids explained their science projects and conducted experiments. They talked about their "heavenly journal" and told how they had proved the treasure legend wrong. Their neatest themes and best artwork were on display. They presented a play they had written which had a speaking part for every student. They served punch they had made and cookies they had mixed and baked in the apartment.

Last of all, Mom handed out the individual report cards. Everybody except Travis passed to the next grade. He skipped to sixth, putting Lily into a pout because they would no longer be in the same class. Sam reminded her that they'd still be in the same room, which, after she considered it, seemed to be acceptable.

"I won't be here," Hank said. "I'm going to a real school, in town, next year."

"Me too," Mack echoed. "We'll play football and have proms. The real thing."

Page thought the regretful look in their eyes denied the proud words. Lack of reaction from the other kids seemed to disappoint them. Lately the boys had behaved well and seemed interested in school, except when their parents were around. Then they acted bored and superior. Probably their parents held onto the grudges and kept the ill will alive. Page resisted sympathy for the boys.

As soon as Hank and Mack had their report cards in hand, their parents took them away. The others lingered, laughing and talking and telling Mom they hoped she'd be teacher next year. Page found one of the twins on the porch, his hands in his pockets, looking in the direction of Comanche Butte.

"Remember my second day here—we went hiking? Seems like a long time ago," she said.

"Yeah," he said. "You sure were ignorant." He laughed. "You didn't mind the bird guts though."

Page nodded. She surely had been ignorant. She had forgotten the agate that one of the twins had dropped in her hand on her first hike to Comanche Butte. On that same day the brothers had challenged her to tell them apart. With everything that had happened this year the memory of those taunting green eyes had faded along with her vow to solve the mystery. Now she turned to him and said, "I haven't discovered—" The afternoon sun shone full in his face, highlighting his lively brown eyes. Brown eyes? Wait a minute! What happened to those green eyes she had looked into at Comanche Butte?

"Where's your brother?" she demanded. Rushing inside, she found the other twin showing his parents a book Mom had bought that told about meteorites in the Big Bend. Just as Page came near, Mrs. Powell glanced around the room and said, "Where did Bret go?"

Aha! thought Page. Bret is brown-eyed, "br" for brown. That's how I can remember. Why didn't I notice? Heading out again to the porch where Bret was throwing rocks toward the back of the playground, she called triumphantly, "Bret, your parents are looking for you."

"Aw shucks," he said. "How'd you know?"

"That's for me to know and you to find out," she said, echoing their flip answer to her question at Comanche Butte. She laughed so hard at his disgusted expression she had to hold onto a post.

He was going through the door when she managed to say, "I won't tell anybody—except Allis." She wished her friend could be here for this celebration. Allis would be glad to know that Hank and Mack would not be in the Panther Flat school next year.

I might not be either, Page realized. She didn't know whether the board would rehire Mom, especially after last night. She knew that they were too fair-minded to blame Mom for what happened, but still she felt doubtful.

After the last vehicle drove away, Page began her usual cleanup while Mom redid her reports summing up the 1953-1954 school year for the board meeting that night. They were both tired and had little to say except to agree that the day was a success. Page couldn't resist asking, "If they offer you the school next year will you take it?"

Mom looked off toward the Dead Horse Mountains for a long while. "What do you think?" she asked. "Has it been too hard having me for a teacher? Has it been too hard having so little living space?"

"It's okay," she said. "More than okay, really. I would be sorry to leave. Anyway, where could we go?"

Mom laughed. "We'd have to find a place. And I believe we could."

"Yes," said Page stoutly, "I'm sure we could."

The board members came soon after supper. The meeting didn't last long. As with other board meetings, Page could hear their voices but couldn't understand what they said. Unlike other meetings, however, they laughed a lot. She heard them leave, and then Mom came in smiling. "Oh, Page! They not only offered me the job again next year, but they're going to hire another teacher to help me!"

"Another teacher! But we'll have two less kids," Page said.

"We'll have several more students. A motel and

some shops are to be built outside the park. The workers' children will come to our school. Won't that be fun?"

With the assurance of a summer just beginning in the Big Bend, and the promise of another school year here, Page made plans to do many things. She congratulated herself on solving the mystery of the twins, but she felt a bit chagrined that she hadn't done it sooner. Now she had to see Alsate. The Apache chief, who was so plain to everyone else, had eluded her all year. Another summer adventure would be getting to know the family scheduled to move into Allis's former house. They had a boy who would be in Page's grade— seventh next year—and a girl Margaret's age. They were coming from a national park in the North Dakota Badlands, another new place to learn about.

Page intended to write Allis the news, including the promise of riding lessons with Doug and her suspicions that Hank and Mack weren't really happy about moving to the town school.

When Allis had first gone away, she had written how she longed to be back in the Big Bend. She complained about the cold weather in Maine, but admitted she liked the skiing. As Margaret had hoped, Allis had seen moose and had been impressed. She enjoyed crossing the border to visit Canada, a very different experience from crossing the border into Mexico. As time passed Page could tell Allis was growing happier just as she herself had in the Big Bend.

The next day Page forgot letter-writing when Gypsy Meg and Margaret rolled to a stop at the back door in their pickup. Margaret stumbled out shouting,

"Page! Come home with us. Grandma gave Carmencita away, and she's leaving next week. Can you come?"

Gypsy Meg clambered down from the truck cab. "I had to do it," she said to Mom. "The government's been bugging me about keeping her in captivity. But I can't just turn her loose."

Page couldn't believe it. "What've you done?"

"Gave her to a zoo," Margaret lamented.

"The San Antonio zoo," Gypsy Meg added. "Near enough so we can go visit her." Page had never seen her so glum. "It's best for Carmencita. They're building a special habitat for her, like she'd have in the wild."

"Just one more week with Carmencita," Margaret said, shaking Page to make her understand.

"We'll wait here if you want to get your things," Gypsy Meg offered.

Inside, Page threw herself on the sofa, crying. "Mom, I can't go. I don't want to say good-bye to her. I can't, can't, can't!"

Mom sat beside her, holding her hand. "Yes, you can. This past year you've overcome harder things than saying good-bye to Carmencita. And you can help Margaret say good-bye to her, just as you've helped me so many times."

After a while, Page sat up and wiped her eyes. "Maybe I'll take my new horse books. Margaret needs to know about horses so she can ride with Doug and me this summer. What did I do with my suitcase?"

In less than fifteen minutes, she was bumping along the road to the river with Gypsy Meg and Margaret. She felt a tingling excitement tempered with sadness. Back of them on the lodge road lay Alsate waiting for her to discover him. Ahead of them on the Mexican border, waited Gypsy Meg's "Lion of God." We'll have a week with Carmencita, Page thought. We'll make every day count.

Acknowledgments

The author drew information from the many letters she wrote during 1952–1954 while she lived at Panther Junction, Big Bend National Park, Texas.

Brown, Vinson. *How to Understand Animal Talk*. Boston: Little, Brown, 1958.

Carpenter, Allan. *The Encyclopedia of the Central West*. New York: Facts on File, 1990.

Horgan, Paul. *Great River: The Rio Grande in North American History*. Vols. 1 and 2. New York: Rinehart, 1954.

Langford, J. O., with Fred Gipson. *Big Bend: A Homesteader's Story*. Austin: University of Texas Press, 1952.

Maxwell, Helen. *A Guide for the Big Bend*. Marathon, Tex.: Big Bend National Park, 1950.

McMillan, George. *The Golden Book of Horses*. New York: Golden Press, 1968.

Pirtle III, Caleb. "Big Bend: Lonely Sentry of the Desert," *Southern Living* (February 1972): 42–49, 66.

Tyler, Ronnie C. *The Big Bend: A History of the Last Texas Frontier*. Washington, D.C.: Office of Publications, National Park Service, U.S. Department of the Interior, U.S. Government Printing Office, 1975.

AILEEN KILGORE HENDERSON grew up in Alabama, where she resides in Brookwood. She served in the Women's Army Corps during World War II as an airplane engine mechanic and a photo lab technician. After the war she graduated from the University of Alabama and taught school in Northport, Alabama; Big Bend National Park, Texas; and Stillwater, Minnesota. She has worked with children and adults as a docent in historical museums and art museums, and she has volunteered at a home for abused women and children. She is a volunteer proofreader for *Alabama Heritage Magazine* and is an active member of the University Lutheran Church. Her first book for children, *The Summer of the Bonepile Monster,* won the Milkweed Prize for Children's Literature and the Alabama Library Association Award. Her second book for children, *The Monkey Thief*, was selected for the New York Public Library's list of 1998 Books for the Teen Age.

Interior design by Will Powers. Typeset in ITC Stone Serif by Stanton Publication Services, Inc. Printed on acid-free 55# Odyssey paper by Friesen Corporation.

More Books from Milkweed Editions

If you enjoyed this book, you will also want to read these other Milkweed novels:

Gildaen, The Heroic Adventures of a Most Unusual Rabbit
by Emilie Buchwald
***Chicago Tribune* Book Festival Award**,
Best Book for Ages 9–12

Gildaen is befriended by a mysterious being who has lost his memory but not the ability to change shape at will. Together they accept the perilous task of thwarting the evil sorcerer, Grimald, in this tale of magic, villainy, and heroism.

No Place
by Kay Haugaard

Arturo Morales and his fellow sixth-grade classmates decide to improve their neighborhood and their lives by building a park in their otherwise concrete, inner-city Los Angeles barrio. The kids are challenged by their teachers to figure out what it would take to transform the neighborhood junkyard into a clean, safe place for children to play. Despite their parents' skepticism and the threat of street gangs, Arturo and his classmates struggle to prove that the actions of individuals—even kids—can make a difference.

The Gumma Wars
by David Haynes
from the West 7th Wildcats Series

Larry "Lu" Underwood and his fellow West 7th Wildcats have been looking forward to Tony Rodriguez's birthday fiesta all year—only to discover that Lu must also spend the day with his two feuding "gummas," the name he gave his grandmothers when he was just learning to talk. The two "gummas," Gumma Jackson and Gumma Underwood, are hostile to one another, especially when it comes to claiming the affection of their only grandson. On the action-packed day of Tony's birthday, Lu, a friend, and the gummas find themselves exploring the sights of Minneapolis and St. Paul—and even find themselves enjoying each other's company.

Business As Usual
by David Haynes
from the West 7th Wildcats Series

In Mr. Harrison's sixth-grade class, the West 7th Wildcats must learn how to run a business. Kevin Olsen, one of the Wildcats as well as the class clown, is forced out of the Wildcats group and into an unwilling alliance working in a group with the Wildcats' nemesis, Jenny Pederson. In the process of making staggering amounts of cookies for Marketplace Day, the classmates venture into the realm of free enterprise, discovering more than they imagined about business, the world, and themselves.

The Monkey Thief
by Aileen Kilgore Henderson
New York Public Library Best Books of the Year:
"Books for the Teen Age."

Twelve-year-old Steve Hanson is sent to Costa Rica for eight months to live with his uncle. There he discovers a world completely unlike anything he can see from the cushions of his couch back home, a world filled with giant trees and insects, mysterious sounds, and the constant companionship of monkeys swinging in the branches overhead. When Steve hatches a plan to capture a monkey for himself, his quest for a pet leads him into dangerous territory. It will take all of Steve's survival skills—and the help of his new friends—to get him out of trouble.

The Summer of the Bonepile Monster
by Aileen Kilgore Henderson
Milkweed Prize for Children's Literature
Alabama Library Association
1996 Juvenile/Young Adult Award

Eleven-year-old Hollis Orr has been sent to spend the summer with Grancy, his father's grandmother, in rural Dolliver, Alabama, while his parents "work things out." As summer begins, Hollis encounters a road called Bonepile Hollow, barred by a gate and a real skull and bones mounted on a board. "Things that go down that road don't ever come back," he is told. Thus begins the mystery that plunges Hollis into real danger.

I Am Lavina Cumming
by Susan Lowell
Mountains & Plains Booksellers Association Award
***Hungry Mind Review* Children's Books of Distinction**

In 1905, ten-year-old Lavina is sent from her home on the Bosque Ranch in Arizona Territory to live with her aunt in the city of Santa Cruz, California. Armed with the Cumming family motto, "Courage," Lavina deals with a new school, homesickness, a very spoiled cousin, an earthquake, and a big decision about her future.

The Boy with Paper Wings
by Susan Lowell

Confined to bed with a viral fever, eleven-year-old Paul sails a paper airplane into his closet and propels himself into mysterious and dangerous realms in this exciting and fantastical adventure. Paul finds himself trapped in the military diorama on his closet floor, out to stop the evil commander, KRON. Armed only with paper and the knowledge of how to fold it, Paul uses his imagination and courage to find his way out of dilemmas and disasters.

The Secret of the Ruby Ring
by Yvonne MacGrory
Winner of Ireland's Bisto "Book of the Year" Award

Lucy gets a very special birthday present, a star ruby ring, from her grandmother and finds herself trans-ported to Langley Castle in the Ireland of 1885. At first, she is intrigued by castle life, in which she is the lowliest servant, until she loses the ruby ring and her only way home.

A Bride for Anna's Papa
by Isabel R. Marvin
Milkweed Prize for Children's Literature

Life on Minnesota's iron range in 1907 is not easy for thirteen-year-old Anna Kallio. Her mother's death has left Anna to take care of the house, her young brother, and her father, a blacksmith in the dangerous iron mines. So she and her brother plot to find their father a new wife, even attempting to arrange a match with one of the "mail order" brides arriving from Finland.

Minnie
by Annie M. G. Schmidt
**Winner of the Netherlands' Silver Pencil Prize
as One of the Best Books of the Year**

Miss Minnie is a cat. Or rather, she *was* a cat. She is now a human, and she's not at all happy to be one. As Minnie tries to find and reverse the cause of her transformation, she brings her reporter friend, Mr. Tibbs, news from the cats' gossip hotline—including revealing information that one of the town's most prominent citizens is not the animal lover he appears to be.

The Dog with Golden Eyes
by Frances Wilbur
Milkweed Prize for Children's Literature

Many girls dream of owning a dog of their own, but Cassie's wish for one takes an unexpected turn in this contemporary tale of friendship and growing up. Thirteen-year-old Cassie is lonely, bored, and feeling friendless when a large, beautiful dog appears one day in her suburban backyard. Cassie wants to adopt the dog, but as she learns more about him, she realizes that she is, in fact, caring for a full-grown Arctic wolf. As she attempts to protect the wolf from urban dangers, Cassie discovers that she possesses strengths and resources she never imagined.

Behind the Bedroom Wall
by Laura E. Williams
Milkweed Prize for Children's Literature

It is 1942. Thirteen-year-old Korinna Rehme is an active member of her local *Jungmädel,* a Nazi youth group, along with many of her friends. Korinna's parents, however, secretly are members of an underground group providing a means of escape to the Jews of their city and are, in fact, hiding a refugee family behind the wall of Korinna's bedroom. As she comes to know the family, and their young daughter, her sympathies begin to turn. But when someone tips off the Gestapo, loyalties are put to the test and Korinna must decide in what she believes and in whom she trusts.

Milkweed Editions publishes with the intention of making a humane impact on society, in the belief that literature is a transformative art uniquely able to convey the essential experiences of the human heart and spirit.

To that end, Milkweed publishes distinctive voices of literary merit in handsomely designed, visually dynamic books, exploring the ethical, cultural, and esthetic issues that free societies need continually to address.

Milkweed Editions is a not-for-profit press.